ANGELS WITH BRUISES

Thirty Nine Modern Tales

ANDREW
BAGULEY
&
JANET
RAWSON

Contents

About the Authors

Andrew Baguley is a writer, voice artist and actor. He's interested in futures, trends and the twisted thought processes of twenty first century males. He lives in London.

Janet Rawson is a writer, playwright and actor. One of her published plays, 'Mopsy, Flopsy and Death' has been performed in the UK with the German translation produced in Vienna. She lives in Southsea.

Visit our Facebook page "Angels With Bruises Short Stories"

The New Jesus

By
Andrew

I've always been interested in the idea of human evolution. And just because we can't see it doesn't mean it's stopped. Plus, London is definitely going to flood one day, right?

I first met the man who saved my life when my editor told me to interview the new Jesus.

"Some nutcase who apparently is the latest messiah on the block," my editor said. Well, at least it was different from the usual tenants association meetings and complaints about the binmen.

Heading to the 1960s estate I pondered my approach. Perhaps a few lines from the Bible, maybe Genesis. "In the beginning, in New Cross..." It just needed the right mix of humour and cynicism to keep *The South East London Shopping Times* readers happy. And cynicism was my specialty.

The estate was grim and cold on the wet November morning. They should have pulled it down years ago. There'd been a fatal stabbing of a child around the time I joined the paper so it had been all hands on deck. Even some of the Nationals had turned up and stayed for at least an hour. And after the inevitable promises by local politicians, life went on as usual. If anything the place looked more downhearted than before.

Heavy steps greeted my ding-dong and the doorway was filled by an extra large black lady in her forties. The hallways in these flats were narrow, but with her in the way, I was surprised anything, even air, could squeeze around the side. She looked at me sullenly, but then said in a surprisingly sweet voice: "You dare write anything bad or make fun..." The implied threat against the gentle voice made me smile, the natural one I have when I'm not being a bastard or wanting something. The smile that's helped me into many beds in the past. It worked it's reliable magic here, eliciting a giggle from the door blocker and a welcome into the dark corridor.

I was ushered into the kitchen where two other ladies were cooking rice in big pots and a sweet tea was pushed into my hand. "Him jus wake," explained the smaller elderly lady. "Him always brighter in the morning before tings dem a vex him." Well this fits a pattern I thought. Every self-respecting messiah should have a bit of harem action going on, even if the girls concerned didn't exactly make my fantasy top ten.

"Ladies," I said, "you know I'm from the paper, so I have to ask you – what's the story here? What is it about this man that has you running around like domestic goddesses?" The last bit made them laugh – a bit of flattery always goes a long way in my game. This time it was the third lady, a white woman who had seen some hard years and a lot of cigarettes.

"He's real," she said, "there's no shit, he just loves you, whoever you are."

"And he knows stuff," interjected door blocker. "He knows what's going to happen."

"You mean like who's going to win the 2.30 at Newmarket?" Wrong thing to say, but my being able to charm women always had a short shelf life. I thought I'd lost them, but then the white one piped up again. "Please. Just be kind. He'll be kind to you. And about what he says about the flood – I believe him. No doubt." The other women nodded. Flood! What next? A plague of cockroaches? Now that I could believe.

"The first newspaper man." I turned around and there he was. Normally, I would have come back with a quip about being the 'Last Newspaper man' but something stopped me. Maybe it was his gaze – clear dark eyes regarding me and somehow softening all the hard skin it had taken me years to grow. What he said next surprised me. "I need your help or a lot of people will die." Not said in a psycho killer way, but matter-of-fact. "Come next door and I'll explain."

So if you were imagining a Gandhi like set-up, you'd be disappointed. Nothing weird or freaky. A large TV, saggy sofa and some dying flowers in an empty beer bottle. Looked like he'd been sleeping on the sofa as an old yellow duvet was roughly folded and squeezed in a corner. No beads, incense or sandals in sight. He noted my appraisal of the room. "Not my place," he said. "My neighbours wanted me to leave so these women have given me shelter."

"Leave? So you just left? No Police? No fight back?"

"I won't fight. It won't help."

"What, so you believe God will provide?"

"I don't believe in God."

Now this was a new twist. "So how can I interview the New Jesus if he doesn't believe in God? Give me a break here – I've got to do a thousand words on you by 4pm."

"Just a thousand? That won't be nearly enough."

Then he gave me this winning smile and that's when I fell in love with him. Not in a gay way. Heaven forefend. I don't mind what people get up to at home, but not in my backyard. If you get my drift.

"My name is Thomas. That's four words for you to start with." The smile stayed and I got a good chance to take him in.

Mixed race, maybe? Difficult to tell. Olive skin, slim build. Looked like he could do with feeding up a bit, but nothing to call the doc about. Five elevenish. Wearing a cheap T-shirt, loose jeans and socks I didn't want to look at too closely. Age was tricky. From a distance maybe thirty, but when you looked at the face maybe ten years older – or younger. Something about the whole package made me stop dead.

You know how most people carry a tension, a well-worn mark of the wounds they've suffered over the years. The way they hold their body, set their mouth or seed their voice with attack or defence? Well, Thomas was an Alexander therapist's wet dream. He seemed to be at peace, calm, in the moment. No threat, no pain. Nothing was held at bay. The nearest I'd got to anybody like that was when I held my son fresh out of the womb. Before life got in the way. Before I fucked it all up.

But I had too much newsman's DNA in my system not to be totally overwhelmed. I had a story to write. "What's all this about everybody dying?"

"London will flood. The city won't be ready. Many will die."

"Will I die?" Not a usual newsman's question I admit.

That smile again. "One day."

"Now you're being a tease." God what was I saying? The only time I ever used that line was when I was closing in for the kill.

I tried to focus, but it was those eyes and the soft accepting gaze. I looked away in an attempt to regroup. "You've heard of the Thames Barrier, I suppose?" This was London's 1980s concrete and hydraulic response to flooding fears. It even had a tourist café.

"It won't be enough. The river will flood. The sea will come. People will die."

"So you said. But I need a hook. What's your hit rate on predictions? And if it's any good why aren't you sitting in Chelsea with your lottery millions?"

"He told Emma she had cancer and she did." Another voice. I looked around and realised we had an audience. In fact, the tiny room now held about eight people. All women over forty. How did they get in without me noticing? I must be off my game. The speaker was the smoky white woman from the kitchen encounter. "Thomas smelt it on her skin." There was a general murmur of assent. This was getting kinky. "The first time he met her he told her to go to the doctor and get him to look at her breast. She did, and they got it just in time. If he hadn't told her, she'd be dead by now."

"That's what I do. I see things and I try to save." As the man called Thomas spoke, the room stilled once more. "I tried to live my life but I'm different. People get frightened. So I stopped fighting against what I am and with the aid of my friends here I do my best to help. It's all I have left." A pause and then the sound of sobbing. I looked round to see several of the women in tears.

An angry voice. "People are just bastards. The things they've done to him. They don't deserve to be saved." Now this was more like it; a slim Asian looking lady wearing a tight blouse and flushed with passion. Maybe being the New Jesus had its up side.

"We all are who we are Marsha. We are all in pain and we do what we do. Whatever we do is the best we can do. We all are worthy of redemption and if I can save just one person I will." Thomas' mini sermon sounded a bit New Age to me, but it certainly had its effect on Marsha.

"I'm sorry Thomas. But they've been so unfair…" She looked even more becoming as her eyes filled with tears and she tried to catch her breath. Jesus! A room full of weeping women and me the wrong side of the door. That was when Thomas saved me for the first time. He raised himself from his saggy sofa throne, pulled me up from the ratty wicker pouf where I'd been sitting, and hugged me. I can't remember the last time I'd been this close to a man. For an instant I pushed back but then felt a wave of love come over me. Tears tried to form in some lost desert region of my body. Fighting them down, I whispered: "Thomas… can you smell anything… on me?" Thomas pulled gently back and looked at me, beyond my eyes. That smile again. "Only cigarettes."

I don't know how I got back to the office. But there I was, sitting blankly at my hot desk when the bulk of my editor arrived.

"What's up Jack? Have you been saved?"

"Uh, what, yes. How did you know?"

He looked at me strangely, trying to find the Jack he knew and despised. "The story Jack. Is it a runner? If so, I need it pronto and unless they've installed telepathic PCs while I was at lunch there doesn't seem to be much going on here. In which case I need some quick puff for Property pages on Lewisham bucking the house price trend. Er, now? Or do I have to say please?"

"London's going to flood. People will die. We have to warn them."

"Hello? Anybody in?" He waved a stubby finger at his head.

"I'm just saying what Thomas said." Normally, I wasn't so lame. But today it just wasn't in me. I was at his mercy. Maybe some of the New Jesus dust was still on me, for he surveyeth his minion from the mountain and spake nice words.

"Jack, leave it. I know a shit storm when I hear one. Just give me two hundred words on housing hotspots and go home." And with that, he waddled back to his own world.

I had a troubled night. The cable porn and vodka didn't help the sleep come this time. After I turned the TV off, I just sat there in the dark for a long while, thinking and doing nothing.

Some of the old Jack was back the next day. But it took over a week to return to full bastardisation. The editor was right, of course. What could we possibly do with this story? I thought of calling *The Fortean Times* but I knew that would only make things worse for Thomas. Only a few conspiracy theorists would believe the flooding bit. And if you put it about that the man could smell disease, that little council flat would become a madhouse.

I did speak to him twice more though, before the end. He'd given me the mobile number of one of the women, in case I wanted to ask more questions. I'd hoped it was Marsha's number, so I called it. It wasn't. When I got through to Thomas, he sounded sad and distant.

"Thomas, this flood. When will it happen?"

"I can't say. Tomorrow. Next week. Next year. But it will happen."

"I'm sorry Thomas. I don't think I can really help you with your story. It's all a bit too much for us. Maybe another paper..."

"I understand." Then the door dinged in the background and he was gone.

The year turned into next. I don't really know where the minutes and the hours went. The new woman in Classifieds helped me to pass some of them. And when I allowed the seconds to be counted, I still thought about Thomas. Maybe I slept just a little better. But from late spring onwards, it all started to go crazy. We'd had a mild wet winter, but as soon as June hit, London began a heatwave like even the editor couldn't remember. The mercury hit 45 C most days – that's 110 plus in the old money. The elderly dropped like flies. There was a general sense of panic in the air. Was this really the start of the climate change they'd all been bullshitting us about for years?

Of course, we didn't touch on that. We were too busy reporting the local madness. Ice cream rage, AirCon rage, Water rage. It was day twenty-four of what we were calling the Microwave Summer when Thomas called me from Lewisham Police Station. For a moment my poor heart fluttered like a teenage girls as I asked him what was going on. Something in me wanted an excuse to see him again.

"I'm in protective custody, and also charged with inciting a riot."

It seemed that word had got out about Thomas' sense of smell. Some sensational reporting from a National paper and a crowd already turned half beast from the heat had gathered outside the flat. They wanted help and when they couldn't all get it, they wanted someone to blame. For everything. Someone was pushed over a balcony. Someone else crushed. Someone shot by the police. I shuddered to imagine the scene inside that crowded flat with the ladies under siege and the wild animals clawing and biting their way in.

"Thomas, I'm coming to get you." I stood, grabbing my car keys, ready for action. But he stopped me.

"Don't. Get out of London. High up. The water is coming. You are the only person I can save."

"Why me?" Too late, there were police voices, and he was gone.

My compassion and rusty sense of injustice got me halfway there before I turned round and drove for high ground. When I reached the Malvern Hills, I realised I'd not even called the woman from Classifieds. I calmed myself in a local pub. It was all nonsense. There wouldn't be a flood.

The heat would go and there would be rain. I could write Property again.

* * *

Some years later, in the camp, I met a beached meteorologist who explained it all rationally. That biblical day, the temperature in the North Sea reached a tipping point. Mixed with warm air from the land, a super cell formed over the Thames estuary. It merged with a similar monster that had developed over the Netherlands and then mutated into a Cat5 hurricane. The weather people were in shock and by the time they issued warnings, a ten-metre storm surge, riding on a high tide, was roaring up the Thames in time for the evening rush hour.

They closed the Barrier, but the 1970s designers hadn't read enough apocalyptic fiction. It didn't hold. The surge bullied its way into Central London leaving devastated suburbs both sides of the river. People drowned on the roads, on the streets, in their comfy safe homes. Men, women, children, pets. The weak, the strong, the mad, the innocent. Those sweltering in stalled tubes had the worst deaths after the lights failed and they couldn't get out. Tens of thousands died in the flood and those who felt themselves lucky to survive were shocked when the hurricane hit, not wanting to be outdone by its surging sibling.

It didn't run out of steam until Swindon, turning the whole Thames estuary into an inland sea. It was all over for London. They tried to rebuild, but the once in ten thousand year event happened again two years later, along with a lot of other crazy weather shit and then, of course, famine. Emergency planning creaked into action and what was left of the government moved into some tunnels in Shropshire. The expected help from Europe and the US never came – they were having their own problems.

Me? Well, nothing can touch me. I'm blessed, don't you know. I live and work in a refugee camp. I act as a sort of PR rep for all the other Thomas types who started to come out of the woodwork after the event. Those who could see the future, smell our sickness and even read minds. Turns out their DNA is slightly different to ours. They're the next stage in human evolution. The version dot 2 of humans. That's what the Chinese scientists say anyway. They've been around all along. Maybe Jesus, Buddha, the lot of 'em. An unpopular theory, so I have to tread the middle ground and keep everyone calm. For once in my life, I do good works and don't mind being one of the obsolescent versions. Maybe I always was obsolescent anyway. Not that my current squeeze is too bothered.

And Thomas? Lewisham was pretty much trashed. All they found in the police station months afterwards were unrecognisable rotting bodies. When I remember that I was the only one he saved, I get down on my knees, tears come freely to my eyes and I begin to pray.

Forty Years

by
Janet

Recuperating from a rotten chest infection on the island of Phu Quoc in Vietnam, I only had the energy to idle away my time people-watching. Us Brits abroad are a wonder in wearing things that we'd never be seen dead in at home! One cheeky item inspired this story.

Mrs Dalgleish waved lazily with one hand whilst shading her eyes with the other. Mr Dalgleish waved lazily back as he stood waist deep, peeing in the crystal waters of the Gulf of Thailand. They had been propelled to take a six-week holiday by the enormity of celebrating forty years of marriage.

They'd always enjoyed travelling, well, what they termed as travelling. A fortnight in a villa in Portugal, or Turkey, or Greece, the odd city-break. But they'd never done this sort of thing before – a long haul flight to a tropical island.

They'd plumped for all-inclusive, so they didn't have to worry about running out of money for food, or drink for that matter. And also, as they rightly assumed, there was an English menu alongside everything else, in case the local dishes proved a little too adventurous in spice and ingredients. Amazement and child-like delight swamped them as they were led through beautiful, well-tended gardens to the verandah of their bungalow with a sea view. On the verandah, there was a cushioned swing for two. Beyond, through the open doors, into the bungalow, two caramel leather recliners, a low coffee table between them, and champagne on ice waiting to be popped.

A rattan room divider separated the living area from where the king-size bed lay strewn with rose petals. To the side of the bed, a large piece of sheet glass through which they could see a luxurious bath, loo and shower.

They'd had a giggle at the bathroom, why would you want to see each other in the altogether doing your business?

Once left alone, Mrs Dalgleish unpacked quickly; she was a devil for order in hotels. Meanwhile, Mr Dalgleish poured them two glasses of bubbly. Not the best they conceded, but it did the job!

Everything was splendid for the first two days, as close to heaven as they thought possible. On Day Three, Mr Dalgleish began to experience a 'gippy' tummy. Mrs Dalgleish dug out their arsenal of English drugs. Was it the diarrhea or sickness he needed pills for? Mr Dalgleish, never known for being a good patient, snarled: 'Both!'

Unfortunately, Mr Dalgleish's gippy tummy showed no signs of abatement over the next few days as Mrs Dalgleish, who had no such symptoms, ate for both of them.

Mr Dalgleish just about had the strength to heave himself from the beachside bungalow to the even closer beach side sunbed, Mrs Dalgleish organising towels and sunscreen, sunglasses and water. But the water made him grumpy as merely a sip would necessitate a speedy retreat to the loo at the back of the bungalow.

On Day Five, Mrs Dalgleish tentatively suggested he see a doctor. Her head was snapped off for her trouble. So she lost herself in a gritty murder mystery on her Kindle.

Mrs Dalgleish took to breakfasting on her own and found herself easily befriended by transient holidaymakers who were only too happy to share adventures over the exciting fare on offer.

On Day Eight, Mr Dalgleish, alone in their bathroom, noticed his face was thinner and his belly appeared smaller. He remembered Mrs Dalgleish pointing at some scales in the bathroom on their arrival and laughingly 'hiding' them in the wardrobe. He was astonished to discover that he'd lost six pounds in a week. He studied his face again; yes, there was a definite suggestion of a jawline and his man boobs didn't appear quite so bouncy. And the beginnings of a tan had made his eyes sparkle bluer.

He replaced the scales and waited for Mrs Dalgleish to come and pack the day-bag for the beach.

Day Ten and Mrs Dalgleish was thoroughly fed-up of his carping and moaning. She daydreamed about committing the perfect murder, then committing it to paper, followed by escaping for a global book-signing tour.

Meanwhile Mr Dalgleish, experiencing an emergence of his younger self couldn't help but view his wife of forty years with a certain growing repulsion. She was fifty-eight and she looked it. He though, with the weight falling off, was beginning to look younger than *his* fifty-eight years. Almost, dare he use the word - yes, virile!

Whereas Mrs Dalgleish, in her large polka dot pink bikini, waddling down to the sea, with a sarong pulled tight under her bust that was dropped at the very last moment before entering the water, had really had her day.

Mrs Dalgleish, attuned to the moods of her husband, silently observed the thoughts that were transparent in his eyes, and wisely decided to say nothing, merely downloading grislier and bloodier murders to while away the sun-drenched days.

Mr Dalgleish, who wasn't a great reader, spent the days fantasising about the way the fit young women adorning the beach kept covertly eyeing him up. And how he could show them a thing or two about British men.

Day Fourteen, Mr Dalgleish was beginning to feel better and snuck to the hotel gym whilst Mrs Dalgleish enjoyed a leisurely breakfast. He was so enamoured of his emerging new body, Mr Dalgleish decided he could manage to skip at least one meal a day.

Their comfortable lovemaking had ceased when he became ill. Mrs Dalgleish had reached out twice in the last few days as she recognised he was well on the mend. The rejection had hurt, but she kept her counsel.

Day Sixteen and Mr Dalgleish was feeling well enough to enjoy an evening meal, but startled Mrs Dalgleish with his strange behaviour. Eventually, she realised he was attempting to flirt with every woman in the vicinity. Female guests moved their chairs to avoid Mr Dalgleish's eye-line. Male waiters only began to serve their table.

Over the next few days, as Mr Dalgleish became a laughing stock, Mrs Dalgleish realised other guests were going out of their way to be kind to her at every opportunity.

By Day Twenty-one, Mrs Dalgleish, desperate to protect her spouse, considered faking a heart attack in order to manoeuvre an earlier flight home. If he was like this now what would he be like on Day Forty?

Mr Dalgleish was unaware of his wife's concerns and equally oblivious to the tide of hostility greeting him every time he set foot inside the dining area. He of the mighty appetite had become a picky eater, steering two pieces of cucumber and a tomato onto his plate for lunch, alongside the thinnest sliver of fish. And once they were consumed, he loudly pronounced how full he was.

At last Mr Dalgleish, eyeing himself in the bathroom mirror on Day Twenty-six, having sent Mrs Dalgleish to breakfast alone again, decided he could detect the beginnings of a six-pack. He had to search hard, he was able to admit to himself, but he could definitely detect an underlying ripple of muscle.

That day, he strongly encouraged his wife to go on one of the scheduled tours. Once free, he escaped to the many beach shops scattered on the roadside between the hotels.

Not finding him on her return from the Pepper Trail (which would have been very boring had she not had the good fortune to meet two Alaskan widowers on the minibus), Mrs Dalgleish ventured onto the beach. She scanned the sunbeds, but he wasn't lying prone on any of them. Anxiety gnawed at her; she'd never known him stray far.

Then to her right, she heard a voice say: 'Get your camera Mand, he's back again!' followed by smothered laughter. Mrs Dalgleish looked toward the shoreline and began heartily wishing that spontaneous combustion was not a thing of fantasy, as Mr Dalgleish strutted into view. He was wearing what Mrs Dalgleish could only describe as budgie-smugglers - very tight, blue and white spotted budgie-smugglers. You could see everything! And one white spot sat clearly on the head of his tiny flaccid penis, his belly round and protruding above it.

Oh the shame! But worse was to follow, as he purposefully strode onwards, a big smile on his face, oblivious to the quiet laughter of the sunbed bathers. With horror, Mrs Dalgleish realised he was wearing a thong!

He looked ludicrous, his fleshy, pale buttock cheeks wobbling about like soggy blancmange. Was he delirious? Had he lost his wits? No, the way he was moving, the way his eyes sought the crowd, made it clear that he thought he was a sex god!

He didn't see Mrs Dalgleish trembling with humiliation and anger. Nor did he see her turn on her heel, tears cascading down her face.

Blushing to her core, Mrs Dalgleish made a dash to their bungalow, hiccupping sobs growing in strength and volume. What to do? What to do? She couldn't cope with facing him at the moment, she couldn't put into words the shame she felt. His strange behavior disgusted her, the misplaced vanity, the monster he had become. She wrote a hurried note, saying she had booked an afternoon tour and didn't know what time she would return.

She scrabbled about in her bag to find her sunglasses, putting them on before rushing out. She didn't know where to go, she didn't want to be seen weeping by anyone. She skulked along a hotel corridor thinking perhaps that she could find a hidey-hole to pull herself together. But when she found herself in reception, she took in the two Alaskans chatting to the tour guide and dove out of the gleaming glass doors into the heat. She couldn't trust herself to chat inconsequential nothingness when the weight of Mr Dalgleish's madness hung so heavy in her mind.

* * *

Mr Dalgleish completed his two full laps of the seafront and began to wend his way back to the bungalow. He wanted to ensure that he was fully covered before Mrs Dalgleish arrived back from her trip. He read her note and snorted, catching a reflection of himself in the glass betwixt bedroom and bathroom. He smiled, turned sideways, raised his arm in a wrestling pose. He looked hot, really hot. He looked like a man half his age, throbbing with sexual power. If he could see it, anybody could! But what to do? What to do with that baggage of a wife? She would scupper his chances with the ladies, sticking alongside him like a limpet.

But while she wasn't here, well, he could play. He dressed carefully, the new shorts cut into him a little, but they'd loosen as he wore them. The sleeveless T-shirt was snug, clinging to his nearly six-pack and really did bring out the youthful twinkle of his eyes. His Old Spice aftershave, which he'd packed but not used until today, gave him the usual manly kick. He struggled into his new turquoise espadrilles, but they were worth the struggle, and picked up his new man-bag. Striking a macho pose before opening the door and sauntering towards the restaurant for lunch, he practised some chat up lines in his mind. 'Plenty more than meat and two veg for lunch here!' Little wink, little smile. 'Ladies, can I service you first?' Little laugh. He'd have them eating out of his hand.

He was disappointed to find the restaurant quite empty, with no single ladies. He helped himself to a sliver of melon and mouthful of salmon mousse and chose a table at the back with a full view of the entrance. He heard, before he saw, the two oversized chaps waddle in. Mr Dalgleish watched with disapproval as they piled their plates to capacity. As they turned, one of them caught his eye.

'Mind if we join you?' he said, plonking his full plate on the table. 'The name's Carter and this here is Logan.' The other man smiled and pulled out a chair.

Mr Dalgleish was livid, this would totally blow his plans! But being English, with years of repression, he heard himself say: 'No, no, do join me.'

But now he was trapped by these two, ugly, fat hulking men. In truth, he felt a little puny beside them, but comforted himself knowing younger women loved a six-pack more than they craved wobbly love handles.

'English?' queried Logan.

'Yes, yes, spot on.'

'Alaskan,' said Carter.

'Oh, Alaska.'

Carter and Logan looked at him, both nodding slowly before murmuring: 'Yep, Alaska.'

'Here on your own?' asked Logan.

Mr Dalgleish hesitated, but forty years of marriage could not be dismissed lightly. 'Ah, no, here with my wife.'

'She's not here?' Carter enquired, looking around as though she might be hiding.

'Oh, no, no, out, on, on a tour.'

'Now holdy-on a little minute here, was she on a tour this morning?' Logan was smiling.

'Yes, I believe she was.'

'The Pepper Tour?' Mr Dalgleish inclined his head slightly. 'With us!' thundered Carter. And then they tumbled over each other:

'What a Lady!'

'Such a sense of humour.'

'She had the whole minibus laughing.'

'A real English... what's the flower?'

'Rose?'

'That's it, Carter. English rose, that's her to a T.'

'Brenda?' Logan directed his question to Mr Dalgleish.

His Brenda? Making everybody laugh? His big Brenda, an English rose? These guys clearly needed glasses.

'You are one lucky man. She talked about you all the time,' Logan continued.

'Telling us this is a very special holiday –'

'Your wedding anniversary –'

'Forty years, right?'

Mr Dalgleish murmured a feeble consent.

Logan leapt in: 'You having a good time here?'

'Yes, yeh.'

'Hey, you've been ill, right?'

'Tummy troubles.'

'We know 'bout them, don't we Logan?'

'Sure do, must have lost pounds in weight.'

'Catching up again now!' They both guffawed.

Meanwhile, Mrs Dalgleish was sitting in a shaded corner of a deck bar in the hotel next door, her sunglasses still glued to her face. She'd stopped crying as the anesthetic properties of a second very generous, very cold dry vodka martini with olive, slid down her throat. Having had no lunch, they hit the spot quickly. Her embarrassment had now shifted to a healthy level of icy rage.

She dug around in her cavernous bag and produced a notebook and pen. She opened it to two empty pages facing each other. On the left she wrote and underlined the word Pros, and on the other, Cons. And began scribbling furiously, but when she needed to turn the page after only a few moments, having run out of space, she was surprised to see her list was all cons and not one pro.

Here she was, knocking on the door of sixty, writing a list, after forty years, about the good and bad points of being married to Mr Dalgleish. She paused her scribbling for a moment to savour another sip of cocktail and look out to the azure sea. This encouraged unbidden thoughts to stray into her mind; thoughts she'd long learnt to push asunder, but now were screaming for attention.

She'd known forever that she was brighter than Mr Dalgleish, more adventurous, more courageous. But she'd deliberately quashed impatience towards her husband, believing marriage was more sacred than her potential pathways in life. She'd stuck at a job way beneath her capabilities, avoiding all opportunities for promotion so that her husband could become the major breadwinner.

She'd told Mr Dalgleish that their inability to become pregnant was probably down to her. She knew full well it was nothing to do with her anatomy, having been thoroughly checked out. And this had been confirmed by the doctor.

Her husband's sperm count was the next test in line and the probable culprit for their issues around infertility. But she'd never wanted to put Mr Dalgleish through that level of humiliation, so she merely accepted children wouldn't be a part of their lives.

Mr Dalgleish was the reason they still lived on the outskirts of Birmingham in a three-bed semi. He'd never had the desire to move out or up. He liked to be kingpin amongst the neighbours, not that he'd admit or even understand this concept. He'd worked for the same firm for forty-two years, been a manager for the last twenty-five and purported he was really happy in the role. Mrs Dalgleish didn't doubt it, he was in a safe place and didn't have to challenge himself.

Mrs Dalgleish had long known that she treated Mr Dalgleish as the child she never had. And, of course, all the while he treated her as a 'wife', she was prepared to ignore his failings and look after his every need. But, as she now acknowledged, if he started mistreating and degrading her, she would not be happy to sublimate her spirit.

Mrs Dalgleish bent her head, picked up her pen and scrawled across both the Pros and Cons, 'WANKER!' She wasn't sure if this was directed at herself or Mr Dalgleish – although Mr Dalgleish was her suspicion.

Finishing and reordering a third vodka martini, Mrs Dalgleish made herself look into the vortex of life without Mr Dalgleish. Could she survive? What would she do? Wasn't she too old for change? Where would she go? What would she do for money?

Rather than filling herself with fear, her thoughts filled her with glee, excitement. She suddenly spied Carter and Logan walk onto the deck, their loud voices piercing the afternoon haze as they ordered two beers. It was Carter who spotted her in the corner.

'Brenda! Need a top-up?'

'No, I'm already on my third!'

'Barman, another of whatever the lady is drinking.'

24

The barman smiled lazily, raised his hand and moved expertly around his bar, before carrying the tray of drinks to the table as the two Alaskans squished themselves into the chairs.

Logan said: 'Just had lunch with your husband.'

'Oh.'

'He thought you were on another tour?'

'Ah.'

'But you're not?'

'No,' said Carter, 'you're here, drinking…?'

'Vodka martinis.'

'Another one on the way!"

'Ooh no, I can't have a fourth.'

'Why, who's goin' tell?' Logan's voice rumbled with suppressed laughter. He went on, 'What you doin' here on your own? If that's not a rude question.'

'Just, um, doing a little bit of thinking.'

'Thinking.' Carter nodded as he repeated her words. 'Everything OK though?'

Brenda couldn't bear the unexpected kindness and burst into tears. She didn't see the look that Logan and Carter passed between them, but she did grab the big chequered handkerchief popped under her dribbling nose.

* * *

Day Twenty-eight found Mr Dalgleish pleading, on his knees, for Mrs Dalgleish to stop packing and sit down and talk to him. Mrs Dalgleish moved around him, gathering her things with a sense of revulsion at his neediness.

'What are you so cross about?' he whimpered. 'Talk to me! Why are you packing? Where are you going?'

'I'm going away.'

'But we have another fourteen days here!'

'I'm not coming home with you.'

'You have to!'

'No, I don't and I'm not, I'm going somewhere else. Today. Yes, I'm going somewhere else today.' A beam spread across her face as her big new adventure beckoned.

'But all your stuff… at home.'

'I can buy new stuff.'

'The house, the garden, the car…'

'All replaceable.'

'Me?'

Mrs Dalgleish declined to answer, and without looking at her husband of forty years, continued packing her toiletries.

'Brenda!'

Mrs Dalgleish zipped her suitcase, looked at her husband with a critical eye, nodded once, set the case on its wheels, picked up her handbag and opened the bungalow door.

'Where are you going? At least tell me that!' Mr Dalgleish pleaded.

Striding away, and without turning her head, Mrs Dalgleish called back: 'Alaska!'

Fat of the Land

By
Janet

Like most women, I have an obsession about body image and fat. But this character's fight with fat has a happy ending.

Being honest with yourself is never easy, is it? But there comes a time, oh yes, there comes a time. For me, that time was between 1.08 and 1.38pm on July 21st 2013.

Our bathroom was upstairs. That was one of the few banes to our idyllic life. Everyone has to use the bathroom, although I must admit, a couple of times when my husband was out, I'd pee in the garden, behind the hydrangea. Didn't seem to do it any harm.

This particular day, I was obviously being well-behaved and had decided to use the bathroom. I gathered my supplies and began the long journey up the stairs. There were twenty-three, which always created a rhythm problem, whether to start on the beat or off the beat. I usually started off the beat as it appealed to me finishing on the word 'Pi'.

Right foot, ces, left foot, per, right foot, fect, left foot, pi, and so on and so forth. Perfect Pisces! Each roundel of two, stop, replenish lost energies, four squares of Cadbury Bournville dark chocolate.

When I reached the top, I stopped to catch my breath, as we didn't have oxygen equipment installed. On this particular day, Friday, when the breathy rattling had subsided, I heard the distinct sound of my husband approaching orgasm. As he'd left for work some hours earlier, I was a little perplexed. I'd waved him off, my bulk hidden behind the front door as usual, just my fistful of fingers in a final farewell.

I crept, as much as my stones allowed, to our open bedroom door and saw my husband's buttocks rising and falling at a rapid rate. I only assume it was the cleaner receiving his pleasures because of the yellow marigolds on the floor and feather duster carelessly flung atop them.

I lumbered away as swiftly and quietly as I could, feeling it only fair to leave them at it.

I squeezed into the bathroom and did my business, ignoring the crack in the toilet seat that I'd executed the previous month. And then, fighting the desire to crawl inside the fridge and demolish its contents, I bravely and noiselessly took myself into one of the spare rooms, the one where I had stacked all the large mirrors.

I hadn't looked at myself full length for five years. I'm glad the bed was there to catch me. I was horrified.

I struggled upright to make another attempt. I looked, truly looked at myself. I was larger than my wildest imaginings. I was elephantine, gross, a spludge, a dollop of humanity, a dung-hill of pockmarks.

My hair lank, unkempt was slapped flat onto my head with grease. In truth, I couldn't remember when I'd last washed it. At my colossal size, hair washing was a major event.

My dress looked what it was, a tent to sleep four. It's gaudy flowers straining to hold together under the mighty volume of my sloppy hips. Who can design size 32 dresses with pride? Nobody, naturally. The unfortunates chosen for the task play jokes and use inappropriate patterned fabric in sweat inducing man-made textiles. Fair enough, I say.

I found the courage to heave and wheeze myself out of my clown costume. It took some time. The examination of myself unsurprisingly didn't get any better. My pants were definitely pants, not knickers or frillies or lingerie. No, these were working, hard-working, practical pants. Huge, shapeless, elastic fraying pants.

My greying bra? The positive aspect was that the ingenuity of engineering and scaffolding was still holding up after the years of abuse from my ever-ballooning breasts.

My body concertinaed in folds around the grim garments.

I unhooked my bra – the last hurdle – with difficulty, my arms too fat to do anything with ease. My breasts hurtled out like two sacks of overladen doughy flour. They fell until they hit the second tyre of my gut and swung out sideways, their only place of escape. I couldn't see the nipples, they pointed defiantly to the floor.

I sat on the bed to grunt out of my pants.

I stood again. I was revolting, truly obscene. I grasped my belly and heaved it heavenwards just to check that I still possessed pubic hair. It was so sparse! I wondered if it was due to an everlasting lack of light.

I lifted my breasts next, one at a time. I was ashamed that the black mark under each wasn't just a tidemark, but a swamp of ripe blackheads, long overdue for the squeezing.

I let go and allowed everything to settle into its own gravitational place and space. I didn't actually look human. My flesh was mottled, purplish white. My skin was puckered and uneven, total cellulite of the body. There were no identifiable female clues, just quivering lumps of full fat flesh.

I then sat, naked on the bed. My options: I could kill myself. Too cowardly. I could confront my husband with my nakedness and ask him to perform the same duty he had rendered to our cleaner. Too high a possibility of rejection. I could look at a diet book. How many times had I tried that before? I could consult a clairvoyant.

Eamon arrived the following day, when I was assured of solitude. He tried to hide his distaste. He needn't have bothered, I'm used to it. I demanded that he ask the spirits if it was possible for me to regain my former beauty.

'What's beautiful?' he parried, arching his camp eyebrows at me. 'Beauty is in the eye of the beholder and all that.'

'I'm beholding me,' I growled, 'I don't see beauty!'

'You've got beautiful nails,' he defended, not wanting to lose ground.

He's right, I do. When our fortunes changed, I gave up housework and afforded myself the luxury of eternal painted nails. The only thing I had managed to keep up. I did them everyday and when my solid stomach got in the way, I had a woman come to the house twice a week to do my toes.

I didn't think Eamon was a very good clairvoyant, he couldn't answer my question. He left huffing because I refused to pay his full fee.

But a wonderful determination had seized me. That afternoon, I plodded up the stairs without chocolate supplies, not to use the bathroom, but to arrange the mirrors all around the spare bedroom. Everywhere I looked, my eye would fall upon an image of grotesque me. I made several visits up and down the stairs that afternoon carrying forgotten candlesticks and candles, aromatic oils, and an old cassette player I rescued from the double garage. I unpacked packages of subliminal tapes and all the positive thinking books my husband studiously and hopefully bought me for birthdays, Christmas', anniversaries, solstice celebrations, full moons, the arrival of Haley's comet – you get my drift. This man had tried.

My temple built, I wrote a list of four laws.

1. I would spend a minimum of two hours a day in there, naked, surrounded by mirrors.
2. I would complete a physical ritual on entering and leaving the temple, which would include climbing up and down the stairs twice.
3. No food would go beyond the threshold.
4. I would relearn, daily, how to love myself again.

I stuck to my vows religiously. It took six months to the day for my husband to notice a change, a year to believe it, eighteen months to allow himself to start hoping and become encouraging, two years before he was one day seized by desire and made clumsy love to me.

But in two years his hair had receded, his paunch was definite rather than a mere suggestion, and his skin was now sagging and sad.

I was chatting to the new gardener about it, the one I hired three weeks ago. Such an understanding, vibrant sort of man.

Defective Girlfriend

By
Andrew

Please don't think I'm a horrible sexist pig after reading this poem. It's just that sometimes, er, men are, well, just not good at, you know, thingy. Communicating.

My girlfriend is defective.
I did consider taking her back,
But the pub I got her from
Is now a Tesco Express,
So clearly that's not going to work.

When I first got her
She would laugh at all my jokes,
But now she just gives me
That Look.
And then after a short pause
Just carries on talking about
Whatever it was she was talking about,
I have no idea what,
As I wasn't listening.

When I first got her
She would look into my eyes
Like one of those little dogs you see people
    with in Paris.
The gaze would be loving and attentive,
And would be on the lookout
To retrieve any metaphorical stick or ball I
    would throw her way.

But now she hardly looks at me at all
And instead just gazes at her new mobile,

Which incidentally
Is always bloody pinging.

When I first got her
She would always want to have sex with me,
Even when I was tired
Which I thought was a bit unreasonable,
Although sometimes I quite liked it
And usually managed to muster up the
        energy
After a Red Bull or two.
But now even when I ask her to have sex,
It's her who is tired
And then she tells me Red Bull makes my
        breath smell,
Which I don't think is evidence of loving
        behaviour.

So,
Even though she is clearly defective,
I'm stuck with her now.
I did try changing her for another one,
But when she found out
She was so mad
It scared me.

My mate Kevin tells me this is perfectly
        normal,
That this is how it goes.
His girlfriend is defective too,
So I had just better get on with it,
Try and be nice to her,
Take up an activity that gets me out of the
        house,
Keep my head down,
And wait for the end.

It is My Estate, This one

By
Andrew

This is pure memory from my time as a Lambeth Council Housing Officer. Well, as pure a memory as memory ever can be.

It is my estate this one. I am its Housing Officer. It is bin day, 1980.

I meet Jock MacMurray, the caretaker. He is a Silk Cut man and as we sit in his kitchen, the sick dirty smell of old smokes crawls across the table. I wonder how his wife can envelop this acrid taste in her arms each night. But, of course, she smokes too. I imagine them lying together in ignorant nasal, carnal bliss, whispering sweet Scottish nothings to each other.

Perhaps Jock finds my odour as repugnant as I find his. Recently, I have discovered Body Shop and I worry I've overdone it. Peaches, avocados and orange blossom conspire to set me in a tropical orchard world, to transport me away from dismal, cold Clapham. Maybe this is why Jock wastes no time in lighting a waterfall fresh Cut of Silk, in a subtle war of aromas between us. This new smoke is richer and flies higher into the air, full of the vigour of youth. Indeed, it's programmed to find my nostrils and flow unashamedly inside in an attempt at smooth seduction. It nearly works, but ultimately can't reach beyond my deep fear of cancerous ends.

Our dance over, Jock and I wander into the narrow walkways for the daily list of broken windows, smashed doors and new squatters. I think of the last days of Rome, the oily barbarians already within, spitting and shitting on all that is good and pure. We reach the first bin shed. Jock pulls open the door and I am nearly overwhelmed by the putrefactive notes of rotting food, soiled nappies and life lived in decay. Its intensity is almost sexual. Jock grasps the oversized wheelie bin and hauls it into the open air. The bin stands there, patiently awaiting its weekly chance of redemption. Returning to the now empty space, Jock shows me where someone blessed with madness has pulled the water pipe clean away from the wall. This hiss of the thin leak fills our ears as we wonder uselessly why any person would do such a pointless thing. I consider how unlikely it is that this deed could possibly advance anyone's existence and their understanding of universal law. Jock doubtless considers the return of capital punishment. No answer comes to either me in my tropical garden or to Jock in his tar and nicotine courtroom. I scratch the precise words required for repair into my surveyor's notebook.

The binmen reversing their great machine towards the refuse shed interrupt my task. Diesel exhaust pushes its way past us; a sticky insidious smell holding no echo of ancient rainforest. Meaty hands grab the big bin and drag it complaining on squeaky wheels towards the hydraulic mechanism. The cheerful profanities of the earthy binmen smooth its passage onto the grabs; then, the compressed air takes a deep breath and hauls its load into the truck's back passage. A great obscene mulching begins as the vehicle enjoys its late breakfast, releasing yet more hidden smells and bringing them in small packages to my middle class nose as if to taunt me. Go home library boy, they seem to be saying to me in the secret language of human waste.

Taking heed I turn away, only to be recalled by a shout from one of the men. A red button is pressed and the truck reluctantly interrupts its meal. We all look in to see a dead tabby kitten; only its front paws and head are visible, as if it were taking a leisurely morning swim on this sea of rubbish. There is a short pause where I foolishly imagine each man present making a moving internal requiem, then the button is stabbed once more and the creature disappears under the surface with one last desperate wave of its tiny paw.

IT IS MY ESTATE, THIS ONE

Later on in my rounds I am reminded of death once again as I sit listening to a bitter old lady in her boiled cabbage kitchen. I can taste the acid in her speech as she monologues about the alien cooking smells of her neighbours. Listening to the spaces between the words, I detect the excremental stench of loneliness, a smell stronger than any other, perfectly pitched for the human condition.

Leaving my estate with a notebook full of hopelessness, I realise I no longer reek of tropical fruits. I too now smell slightly of garbage and death, and I yearn for a re-application of coconut and mango. And yet I know from the hard evidence of my toilet emissions that I too harbor rich and putrid elemental odours that connect me to the world and mark me out as human. Reassured by this thought, I return to my office to engage in anesthetising banter with other Housing Officers. I do belong in the stench, after all.

Our Geoff

By
Janet

Sumo Wrestling on Channel 4 in the 90s – I just loved it, the pomp, the ceremony, the size of the wrestlers and the shortness of the bouts. I so wished it could have been live in the UK. Our Geoff was the next best thing.

To be quite frank, I were somewhat disbelieving when our Geoff told me he were going to become the first British Sumo Wrestler. Me disbelief turned to downright anger when he started demanding a pound of cooked rice every two hours – and mind, this is through the night as well! Thing is, I had me day job at factory to deal with. The last thing I needed were bein' woken every flaming two hour!

Now I should explain. Geoff had been unemployed for two and half year by now and he'd been searching for summat to occupy his mind. He'd tried gardening – not ours – other people's, but he got too many complaints from customers that he was pulling up plants and leaving weeds. Hardly his fault, he'd never done gardening before and we've all got to start somewhere, haven't we? But all the criticism knocked him back a bit.

But he soon picked himself up again. That's one of the things I've always loved about our Geoff, he's a real trier. D'ya know what I mean? Next he tried car mechanics. First car he did, I thought the fella were goin' to murder him. Again, no understanding that it were his first go at car mechanics. How were he to know that you don't connect the coil to the starter motor?

Well, all this time of being out of work, the poor mite had to have some pleasure, so he were a regular visitor to pub most every night time, and lunchtime when he felt the need. Well, of course, his self-esteem were on floor, so he were comfort eating and I suppose comfort drinking. Course wi' no work and no exercise the weight started piling on and before we could turn round, he'd shot up from eleven and half stone to twenty! I didn't mind too much, although I worried about his heart.

So anyway, back to where I started. He suddenly announces it, on a Tuesday night. I know it were Tuesday 'cos I were rushing to get to bingo. Me and me friend have been going for years, but it's always a rush to get home from work, cook tea for family, eat tea, wash up, wash me, change and be there for seven. I mean, I don't knock off work till half five. Still, that's going away from point.

I've just dished up regular Tuesday dinner – chips, sausage, onion rings and beans – and he comes out wi' it!

'I'm going to be first British Sumo Wrestler.'

It weren't just me that found it funny, I thought our Dean were going to choke on a chip he were laughing that much. And our Moira, who's always had a sensible streak, suggested he should start learning Japanese.

Perhaps for the very reason we weren't supportive, it gave Geoff that added push to prove us wrong. He were up before I were next morning. I found him glued in front of television, playing re-runs of Channel Four's Sumo Wrestling programmes, I didn't even know he'd been recording them!

Well, when I get back from work that night, I thought he'd been beaten up. He were black and blue all over! He looked dreadful. I couldn't even hug him to make him feel better, he were that sore. But then I found out the daft ha'porth had done it to himself! He'd moved car out of garage and had been running at wall to 'harden' himself up, like they showed on the Sumo training. Well, I just got mad at him, told him to stop being so stupid.

That were red rag to bull. He were black and blue for following month, so he were obviously carrying on doing it. He got into it more and more. When I refused to get up and cook his pound of rice every two hour, he got up and did it himself. He had to ask me how to turn on stove and all that, but once he got the hang of it, he were away, there were no stopping him. No, he even started doing odd bit of cooking for family, it were great!

But then he stared getting silly wi' it. He started growing his hair. Well, a thirty-six year old man can't go wandering around Oldham wi' long hair, not when he's looking for a job. We had quite a few rows about it, I can tell you. But not as big as the one when I came home from work and he's standing there, sheepish like, his hair jet black and streaks of dye all down his face and neck. Oh, I were that ashamed of him. What would neighbours think? Big sissy, that's what they'd think. 'Course, our Dean thought it were cool and followed suit and what could I do? Precisely, nowt!

I come home one day and as I open door, this horrible smell hits me. I follow me nose to kitchen to find floor covered in peanut oil and Geoff sitting in his undies in middle of it all, trying to put his hair, also smothered in oil, into a sort of top-knot affair. Apparently, getting your hair right is part of being a Sumo. Bit poncy if you ask me, but I kept me mouth shut.

Then another day, I come home to find him in living room wi' Mr Singh's wife, Mrs Singh, and yards and yards of green material, which I later found out were raw silk. It were one of her old saris. He'd only been telling them at corner shop he wanted to be first British Sumo Wrestler and needed some community support, and this is what Mr and Mrs Singh had decided to donate. They thought it would do for the flimsy bit of material he'd need to go round his middle on competition night. I didn't know where to look.

But Geoff – he just carried on. He put notice in local freebie paper about his intentions and before I know it, he's got some Japanese guy as a coach, Yoshi Saki-Something-Or-Other. And the local T'ai Kwondo group have donated their room to him to practice in, in mornings. T'ai Kwondo people call it a dojo – but it's just a room.

Then Geoff decides to go to Unemployment Benefit Office. He manages to sweet talk them. He convinced them that this was his new business, so they started giving him an extra ten-pound a week towards training. Well, before you can turn around, suddenly there's ten overweight, unemployed guys from the local pubs in the vicinity, also training to be Sumos and picking up their extra ten pounds a week!

Bit after this, I were rushing to get to work and phone goes. It's local radio station, *Red Rose*. The DJ, Jimmy Sparky, spoke to our Geoff personally. He'd heard about his campaign to be first British Sumo Wrestler and wondered if he could do his show live from the dojo one day a week, as he felt it would be of interest to local community.

Well, Geoff were bowled over. So every Thursday, Jimmy Sparky would set up and do his lunchtime show in dojo while they were training. Then on Friday lunchtimes, he'd have a phone-in at studios so folks could air their views on the team's chances. 'Course, all the lads had to choose names for themselves. Our Dean chose his Dad's, Rippling Thunder. Goddun' that, in't it?

Boss at factory were great, he'd play radio over tannoy for us so we could keep up wi' it all. I were right proud of our Geoff, having to talk on radio really made him come out of his shell. It were lovely to see him having such a good time again. He were the same as when we first started courting, all laughter and teasing.

Then, early one Saturday morning, our Geoff were out training, Dean were out rollerblading and our Moira was at her Saturday job and doorbell rings. I thought it were Sandra from next door coming round for a natter. I'd just started doing me roots, so I yell downstairs, 'Hang on!' at the top of me lungs. I rush down in me tattiest dressing gown, yank open the door and there's this great big flaming camera pointing right at me. And this woman shoving a microphone up me nose.

'Would I care to express me views on me husband's hobby?'

Well, I slammed door shut, I couldn't think what else to do. I yell to her through letterbox, could I tell her me views in an hour's time? She yells back, also through letterbox, ooh, she were canny, knocked me down to 'alf an hour. But good as her word, she and camera crew disappeared down path.

ANGELS WITH BRUISES

I flew up them stairs, washed me hair, found a posh frock at the back of the wardrobe, put me face on, all in record time.

I were ready for them any road. I opened the door with my best surprised: 'Hello.'

Family were dead impressed when we sat down to watch programme later in day. It were only a little spot, right at end of local news. But even if I do say so meself, I looked fantastic! The phone began ringing soon as it were over. Our Dean beat me to it, he'd just got his first girlfriend, but surprise, surprise, it were for me. It were Mr Yoshi Something-or-Other ringing to congratulate me, and would I do him the honour of being the Team Mascot. Ooh, I were tickled pink. Geoff were furious, said it would interfere wi' his training programme having me around all time, but he simmered down after a couple of days. He's always been one to overreact.

Anyway, the next week, on a Tuesday, I'd just come out of factory gates, when this dapper little Japanese fella comes up to me, bows, introduces himself as Yoshi, and asks if I could possibly accompany him, immediately, to the local newspaper office where he had arranged for me to give an interview, and sorry for such short notice. I couldn't refuse, he asked so politely. I rushed off to find Sandra, tell 'er I were cancelling our bingo evening and rejoined him.

He led the way to this dead sporty red car, a Toyota he said. He opened door for me and helped me in. He smelt so, ooh, 'Oriental' as he leant over to fasten seatbelt for me. He closed door real gentle, smiling at me through window. He put on the dinkiest pair of leather gloves you've ever seen before he started engine. He were so perfect in his tininess, like a proper little male doll.

Interview went smashing! I felt like a Princess, even though I were only in me factory gear. Would I like a tea or coffee? Glass of wine then? I did say yes to wine. Was I comfortable? Perhaps I'd be able to relax more for the interview if I sat on sofa. It were magic.

It were decided that newspaper would approach Council and suggest next World Sumo Championships should be held in Oldham to really try and put us on map again. It were right exciting. Well, Yoshi were that pleased with the way everything went, he invited me to have dinner with him... in his very own restaurant! How could I refuse?

I realise now I should have rung home but I were that excited and giddy wi' everything. Eeh, Yoshi and I had such a giggle when he tried to teach me how to use chopsticks, I were hopeless! He were just feeding me a peanut when the restaurant door burst open and there's our Geoff, larger than life and twice as angry.

'Course he sized up the situation all wrong, but when Geoff's in a temper, he doesn't stop to think. He let out a roar and went straight for Yoshi's neck. Well, Yoshi was suddenly twirling in the air letting out a blood-curdling yell. We didn't know he were a karate expert. His foot catches Geoff on back of his neck, forcing him forward, Geoff put out his hands to save himself and landed on one of me chopsticks, resting on me plate. It ricocheted up and over to the table behind ours, straight into open mouth of a screaming female customer, who chokes and dies.

It were awful, I'm sure you can imagine. Pandemonium. Yoshi tried to give her mouth-to-mouth but it were too late. Woman's partner passed out. Geoff took one long quivering look and did a runner. I went into a state of shock, found a fork and finished me dinner.

Geoff were caught, obviously, far too big to hide, charged and sent down for manslaughter for eight years. Yoshi, with my evidence, was able to plead self-defence.

It were a terrible time all round. But, after a lot of soul searching, Dean, Moira and meself moved to Preston with Yoshi to try to put it all behind us. I still think about our Geoff, but less and less. I just hope he meets a nice woman when he comes out.

Alien Pain

by
Andrew

This is sort of me, really.

I wish when I woke up
I could comfortably relax,
Stretch out my body without a care,
And breathe in deep of the day,
Instead of immediately having to worry
About all sorts of things,
Like fighting the aliens who have invaded
Our beautiful blue home,
Their evil tentacles spreading everywhere,
Their little rat-like faces
Squinting in pleasure
Every time they shoot one of us
With their laser weapons,
Or turn us into sludge
With those other things they have,
While we, the brave resistance,
Fight on using sharpened cutlery,
Especially spoons,
Like how they use them in prisons.
Or so I've heard.

Actually there are no aliens.
It's all in my head.
And even if there were,
Would they really have rat-like faces and
    tentacles?
No.
Not very likely.

ALIEN PAIN

Although you never know.
I wish when I woke up,
I could feel a warm body next to mine.
A beautiful woman,
Curvy, and when she would turn in
    her sleep,
The bedsprings, in love with her like me,
    would sigh gently
While I watched her
Blowing unconscious air out of her mouth.
Actually, this image is going a bit wrong,
She shouldn't really be blowing anything,
And if her mouth was open like that,
She'd probably be dribbling,
Which is disgusting.

Anyway, she would smell of silk,
Whatever that smells like,
In fact, does it have a smell at all
When it comes off the tree
Or out of the worm
Or wherever it comes from?
I'll Google it when I remember,
When I get out of this bed,
Although I think it's unlikely that it comes
    from worms.
I mean if it did who would wear it?
All those people who don't like creepy
    crawlies.
No way they'll put that on their website,
The silk people.

So, now you have a bit of an idea
About what goes through my head.
Not just in the morning when I wake up
But at other times during the day,
When I should be doing other things,

Like writing my novel,
Or making love to my girlfriend.
Hah! I don't have a girlfriend.
You've probably gathered that.
Although I'm not too bad to look at,
Not just after I've woken up obviously,
But later on, when I've had quick wash,
And thought about brushing my teeth.

But this is why I'm writing poetry.
All girls love poems and hopefully poets,
Like Shelly and Byron
And all that lot.
I bet they had girlfriends,
Even though it was in Victorian times,
When they didn't really do that sort
        of thing.

It would be better if I was a tortured poet,
Tortured
By some terrible event in my childhood
Or by the invasion of the aliens
After they zapped my house and killed
        my dog
And my dad,
Whatever,
Just enough to be tortured properly,
Because they say great art comes from pain.

Pain!
Hah!
I eat pain for breakfast.
Although usually I skip breakfast
As I've gotten up too late.
But if I did get up early enough,
I would definitely eat some pain.

ALIEN PAIN

Well
That's me,
This is the kind of rubbish that goes on in
    my head,
Most days,
And is probably the reason why
I don't have a girlfriend,
Or a very good job,
Or much money,
Or many friends.
But at least I have a laptop
So I can write this kind of stuff.

You thought this poem was about to end,
    didn't you?
I sense you shifting uncomfortably in your
    imaginary seats,
Whispering to your alluring companion,
"When is this going to be over?"

Well, don't worry,
It finishes soon,
Although in reality,
I could go on like this indefinitely,
Telling you all the things I think about.

But because time, as sponsored by the
    poetry clock, is running out,
I will leave the ladies reading this
Part of my phone number.
It starts Oh Seven,
And I'll let you guess the rest,
As I've heard you ladies like a mysterious
    man.

ANGELS WITH BRUISES

Right,
I really am finishing this now,
And also I have to go anyway,
As I have my spoon to sharpen.
If I don't come back from my alien killing
    mission
At least I've left this poem for humanity to
    remember me by.
Goodbye cruel world,
And cheerio.

Nine Hundred Hours Of Drinking

by
Andrew

*I've stolen this concept from my good mate Kevin, who really
does do a countdown of drinking events, but after the initial
gloominess has passed we usually have a decent session. We're
currently on six hundred and eight.*

I remember feeling so happy when I met Terry all those
years ago. I'd been doing this Spanish class as a secret way of
meeting women. About week four, this bloke piped up as we
were finishing, and asked if anyone fancied a beer. They were
a miserable lot in that class so in the end it was just me and
the bloke – Terry – who went round the corner. Five pints
later we were mates for life.

A good male mate is a real treasure. Men can turn in
on themselves and go weird so it's important to find sensible
same sex company. Otherwise, you can turn into one of those
lonely ones with notebooks at the end of station platforms.
Terry was a lovely bloke. Like me, he had no interest in
football, was single, and could both listen and talk. Like me,
he considered himself a man of huge unrealised potential. Of
course, we were in our twenties then.

At this first impromptu session, he told me about his
dream of meeting a South American girl and moving to
Buenos Aries. Not a million miles away from my fantasies
of exotic women and foreign parts. During the many boozy
sessions we had in the following years, we discovered a
shared ambition for starting businesses, predicting the next
big thing and making real, proper money.

Time passed and those ideas turned into more realistic
expectations. Then into decent jobs, marriage and kids. But

when Terry and I met we would drink and keep our dreams alive. We tried getting our wives along a couple of times but it never really worked. The only drinking dynamic was Terry and me. By our forties we'd moved onto wine and a good meal. We still ogled the young waitresses and joked about being pervy older men and pretended we didn't really care. Don't get me wrong. We weren't unhappy. We had disposable income and had done well out of rising house prices. We took our families abroad for holidays, although Terry never did make it to South America. We talked endlessly about accepting our lot while not really doing so. More years passed.

It started to go wrong in our early fifties. One evening, after the third glass of red, Terry got a bit morose.

"Do you realise you and me have only got another nine hundred hours of drinking left?"

"That doesn't sound nearly enough. Are you hinting I should buy another bottle?"

"No, I worked it out. I see you about once every six weeks. Nine times a year tops. And our sessions are around four hours, right? So even if we stay healthy and can still get out of the house, we've only got another twenty-five years at the most. That's not even factoring in cancer. So by the time we finish tonight, we'll have just eight hundred and ninety-six hours left."

"Cheer me up, why don't you!"

"I would mate. But you can't argue with the math."

He was right. But I guess it's a way of looking at life. It didn't bother me like it bothered him.

After that night he brought it up every time. In a jokey way, of course. Said he was counting the hours and keeping a log. Then we'd laugh and talk about something else. But from about eight hundred and thirty-two hours down he became a gloom and doom merchant. We were both interested in world affairs but Terry started to get really angry about things.

"What were we doing in Afghanistan and Iraq? How did we mess it up so bad? When did our politicians get so morally corrupt? And the banks – why can't we control them? And is it only me who cares about global warming? Am I the only one to be turning off the tap when I brush my teeth? Six litres of water that wastes. Six litres!"

I worry about these things too. Sometimes. I guess that was why Terry and I could continue to be friends even when he got more intense. Then, Terry got onto his personal survival.

"Climate change – it's here already. Look, we're in a drought again. How long before there's standpipes in the streets? The whole food chain is unsustainable. Do we seriously think this age of plenty can last forever? Don't get me wrong, I'm more tolerant than most, but we've got to do something about these feral kids. I couldn't fight one, let alone a gang. Would be game over. Six of 'em on the train tonight – I only get every tenth word they say and that's a word to describe hurting someone. So how are we ever going to get through to these kids if they can't even talk properly? I mean how can you reason with people like that? Plus, they had one of those pitbull things. Why does everyone have a pitbull? Why can't they get a spaniel for God's sake!"

You get the picture by now. Terry and I went through a bit of a rocky patch as our sessions turned into him ranting and me listening. I even feigned illness once to get out of a drinking session. Then one day, I got a phone call.

"Hey, mate, great news. We're moving up to Scotland."

"What!"

"Yup. Sometimes you just gotta seize the day. Firm were looking for voluntary redundancies, so I went for it. With my savings and downsizing on the house we'll have enough. Now the kids are pretty much off our hands, we should be OK. And Eileen should be able to find a little shop job or something to keep her busy and bring in a bit of spare cash."

Before I could ask him about how Eileen felt about that he was off again.

"We're gonna rent a place on the East Coast, find somewhere that feels right, then buy. They're really forward looking up there – recycling, green energy projects. One of the councils has even ditched all their diesel trucks and replaced them with electric ones. And it's so peaceful. You can drive for miles without seeing a pitbull!"

A few drinking hours later and Terry's intensity ramped up another notch.

"Mate, you really should think about leaving London, you know. It won't take long for things to get really bad in the city if push comes to shove. You've been fed up with your job for ages. Take a leap of faith! Add years to your life!"

I must admit I was tempted. But my Lucy wasn't easy-going like Terry's Eileen. She'd never leave London. And what would I do? Yes, I was fed up with the job. But it was money. I didn't know anything else. And I needed those ten years till retirement to put more money away. The kid's unis were costing a fortune and the mortgage still had to be paid.

I had to give it to Terry. Once he'd made up his mind up, he moved fast. Within a month he was all packed up and ready to go. We went out for a last beer. It was a strange evening. He had the wild eyes of the leaving-London-converted.

"Mate, I feel a thousand times better already. On my last day, I went in to see my boss and told him what a wanker he was. Seriously. And I've not missed work for even a nanosecond. What a total waste of time it all was. Anyway. Move day is Tuesday. I can't wait!"

"So, how many more hours of drinking do you think that you and I have left?" I asked cautiously.

"Well, even more than we thought. If you come up and spend a week or two once I'm settled, we can drink every night for a week!"

A sad part of me knew that was never going to happen. When was I going to get a week free to go up to Scotland? Lucy didn't like the cold and our family holidays were usually planned well in advance. He and I were both in denial. The difficult evening ended with a final rant from Terry.

"Just think, this time next week, no more pitbulls, no more M25, no more hoodies!"

Terry's move day came and went and he called me about a week later to say they were getting nicely settled. It was even better than he'd dreamed. But we didn't talk for long. We were pub friends, not phone friends. I left that sort of thing to the women.

For a week or two I pondered sullenly on getting older and losing my friends. I was grumpy with Lucy, and for a mad moment, I even thought about leaving her. Then I got a call from Eileen. She was in bits.

Apparently, Terry had left his front door (whistling, Eileen said) to go for a bracing country walk and before he'd gone a few yards, he'd been hit by a silent electric refuse truck. Killed outright. Sadly, it seemed the council were already reviewing the whole electric vehicle policy after a spate of silent accidents and were thinking of going back to diesel.

Terry was buried in London and after the funeral I went alone to the pub where we'd met. I toasted him with a silent pint. But I only stayed an hour. It just didn't feel right. The ironic thing is that we'd never have made that nine hundred more hours of drinking anyway.

A couple of years after Terry died everything seemed to fall apart. Major riots, curfews, a hot dusty London after two years of drought. If only I'd moved out of the city when I had the chance. I sometimes fantasise that if Terry was still alive, he and I could be drinking cold beer somewhere, away from all the trouble, and he'd be saying, 'I told you so.'

Well, I'd better go I suppose. They turn the standpipe on in about half an hour and I need to get in the queue. I just hope the hoodie gang aren't charging a tenner a bucket again.

God, I miss Terry and our drinking hours.

Far Fathoms

By
Janet

This story came into my mind during my second ever soak in a Flotation Tank. I was so bowled over by how the sensory deprivation of my first soak intensified my imagination, I promised myself I would capture the content in my second.

My body is a-tremble, show it I must not. Stealing, yes; I did this thing, yes; punishment I must take as a man. Foolish, the rations of water I stole quenched not my thirst. The ropes are crusty harsh with brine, my wrists chafe.

Sorrow I spy in the eyes of my friend, his cruel task to mete out my penalty. His sword holds not a steady line, but kindly pray I will he act. Make my criss-cross chest cuts deep, speedier to pull the hungry sharks for swift end.

Ahh, sword tip makes me sting, quickly look I about, no shine of tears must to be shown. Look I elsewhere for my salvation, the ship she is dried up, top timbers warping. All sailors dried up too, look a-weary, mighty thirst pinching from inside. Good thing, good thing I lucky to escape slow death.

Orders barking, turn I to plank. Concentrate I to walk steady, slow, no falter. I wish Tobias to proudly see me go, so tall stories to home friends be told. Plank springs up to hit my soles, my vittals are awash. Dark shapes skimmy in clear sea, calm sea, sparkling. It will be merciful quick. Call I out to my God: "Be with me!" Launch I self, straight jump, proud. Fear makes imagining through long fall, see I two beauteous faces atop tails. Sailors dreams and nightmares, mermaids of the mind.

Water closes round, over. Habit I hold breath, prolong life of mine for longer. Brief time. Feel I, not see I, sinuous body flick, curl, legs of mine enfolded. Arms tied, cannot fight, cannot stretch towards surface. Yes, quick fast end. Best of deaths to drown, men say. Is any death easier than t'other? Breath all gone, mind awry. "Lord I be with thee!" Ending.

Flicker up my eyes. Heaven? Darkly dull. Hell? Confusion. Face, female staring at me, soft smile on lips, long hair falling upon my skin – feel it I, tantalising. Heaven – sure, heaven I be in. Mouth above eyes of mine moves. Melodious fluted bubble sound, underwater speaking. Shake mine head. Vision still glowing there.

Splash, gone. I be puzzled. Death, this is it? Sit I up, a-gentle of myself. No more wrapped in water, but water all around of me. Eyes feel for light patches, accustom they, mind cannot believe. Must be I in the process of death; why, a journey longer than the human mind envisage.

Sounds drifting, sounds of relax, I think me laughter hears. Happiness. Sit I long-while a-catching up myself. Giant rocks, glitter of urchins encrusted within. Suffusing light, hues of softness, though keep trying to understand its source, I see it not.

Turn I swiftly, splash, surprise sound. Again smiling face of feminine form, lower than I, floating in water canal hewn in rock. Proffering hand gives, I take, what I know not, brackish brown.

Look I disbelievingly, sequinned tail of shimmering scales, colourings of peacock, undulating beneath, only just, the water surface. Eyes of mine travel from fringed fish tail to melding of hips into human form; scale into flesh, tiny waist, hands of mine could encompass, belly button winking. Mind of mine excited, afraid, compelled. Ah, breasts floating heavy, nipples pointed in water cold, slender neck, heavy hair, wet, fanning, smile beautific. Heaven, truly, an angel.

Gone in an instant. See I the silliness of men's imaginings. Hest hold, mistake I, for in hand still have I package. Sniff I. Stench of nothing. Poke I, gives, comes back. Spy closely, moves not, tongue to test, salty, withdraw I speedily.

Afeard I feel a-sudden, swamping I be in loneliness, wish to cry. Tears fall, rain forth, too young to succumb to death, now snared in spirit world. Time of how long? Howl out sound of hurting.

Immediate two tails splash into view. Pitched notes from their sounds bounce on rock face, hands clasp for mine, fingers interlock, wet flesh, both sides against my chest. Aah, scream as salt enters criss-cross cuts. Fleshes withdraw, vocal cooing, I distressed, panicked. Hands wet of water massage my shoulders sad drooping. Tears flow long while, ache for lost life yawing.

Remember self. Stop. Visiting bodies I tentatively touch, explore slowly. Rounded breasts hold weight, slender waists curve into my caress. Hand slips further. Ahh, withdraw, release I, touch I slippery scales, touch I a living fish. Sound waves captive, giggling and light.

Hold, re-begin.

Dawning.

Dead I be not. Nay, never, but captured in another world. Think I as normal. Feel as ever, view as ever I have done. Dawning. Good feeling, bad feeling, know I not. I am alive. Good. Yes, be this good. World I know nothing of is saviour to my life.

Maids of mer bring me back to self, now and here. Attempts at speech linking. Another language, foreign to mine senses. Time, healer of time. Lesson of patience, keep my strength.

Essence of time dissipated here in the world of undersea. How long here I know not. I know I be the only living creature with no tail. Have touched many tails, many fingers and tails have touched me. Many bubbles of amaze have courted mine thoughts.

Canals of seawater criss-cross my walking path. Exploring, always be I encouraged. Found house of intoxication, mermen, mermaids on underwater stools, tails flapping, body top leaning from the water, drinking shells filled with brain poison. At these places, melodious laughter crashes to crescendo. Long I for ships rum, so to infuse my mind along avenues of escape and forget. Drunk they float by design not desire. Poseidon, their God, be he. I wonder often, as angry in judgement as ours?

I held in world of silence as we link not in words. Kindliness extended always, but to a pet, a trinket. I sad to soul of me.

Ending. No beginnings.

How long now? I know not life from death. Heart cries out in wretched aloneness.

Then thoughts confuse. Ungrateful. I am saved! Saved for why, for what?

Stumble across surprises always. Matriarch's rule, watch I as they organise and sort. The mermen do all their bidding. Relax time a-plenty, music play they, harps and shells, laughter all the time. Love time all places. The shes decide, swell, shimmer passion pure, open their scales, fluted fins of yellow, blue, vulvas bright red, hunger pulls the mermen in.

The love dance always long-time, coquette of teasing before completion, giving, possessing, purity of lust. I watch many times, they mind not, nay arrange my audience. Why? To drive me wild? To make me mad? Nay, loneliness makes the madness in me. My heart is sore. Misses much, friends of my race. How long here I have been?

Perhaps purgatory be its title. Yes, I be in purgatory of the soul. No record have I of time, no chance to judge by seasons passing, no conception of length of stay.

I alone do feel. I long the bait of shark to have been. Wrong is that I question, always. My life prolonged, yes. Remember I holding breath to longer live, and that but a moment. Now this place have I been many long-time.

I wish for death. I observe, outside all time. These creatures and I touch not by heart. I long, I desire but can no merman be, therefore, no part play I in this citadel. Nor can I escape my prison in the huge base sea. Nay, now I be captured truly 'till I die.

For that ending God hope I. May it speed it soon.

The Threshing Circle

by
Andrew

There's a wonderful, tiny village in the mountains in Spain where I did a big, wonderful writing course and this story comes from there, where there is a real threshing circle. Otherwise, I never would have dreamt of writing about a threshing circle. There's none in Lewisham.

She stood on the raised edge of the threshing circle and drank in the land – the majestic bare rock of the mountain that had remained unchanged since the day the world was born, the scrubby trees walking upwards but struggling to gain purchase in the cruel soil, and the sound, more distant now, of pure rich water scampering in the valley far below. She loved this land, it was her land, and she had ranged all over it, planting here, picking there, learning from her mother, and her mother before that.

Just a few feet away was the tree she had loved to climb as a girl. She would hide in its upper branches and watch the villagers thresh the wheat. The chaff would blizzard away and then settle down the slope like yellow snow. She almost smiled. She was the chaff now, the useless thing to be discarded. In a few minutes, no one here would know that the leaves of her tree, picked in springtime and boiled for three days, would make a bitter pregnancy tea to ease the pain of childbirth and help bring forth mother milk.

She looked around the group of men in the circle. There was Donas, crippled now, yet still a commanding presence. She remembered tramping over the hard sloping rocks for two days, looking for the small purple flower that grew only in the cracks between the silver and brown bands of ground. When it was crushed and mixed with the abundant green herb that everyone thought was a weed, it had helped ease the passing of Donas's brother when the growth inside him had become too much to bear.

And there was Marto, looking strong and beautiful and proud, leaning on his scythe as if he was merely about to tend his crop. Marto would never know that many years ago she had lain with his grandfather in a secret place down near the rivers edge, where rampant vegetation had tickled their backs as they made love in a hollowed out space on the forest floor.

Straining her head as far as the two men holding her would allow, she could just see the pathway that led to the cool place near the bubbly spring. She wished she was there now, even though the spring had dried and the surrounding trees were dying of thirst.

Taking a deep breath, she looked around for a final time. It was nearly dusk and peace was settling on the valley. The first bats were about their business, flitting this way and that, harvesting the insects that still buzzed and hummed.

The men of the valley were nearly done talking. They had decided that she, the almost outsider witch woman, was to blame for the drought that had gripped the land for the past six seasons. Crops had failed, babies had died, goats had become barren. But she knew from listening to her mother, and to her mother's mother, that sometimes the rains just stopped. No one knew why, but she had an idea that everything in the world was connected together and somehow things happening in one place could make other things happen in another. Rains would come again, she knew. Life would go back to normal, and she would be forgotten.

Donas banged his stick. The men stilled. It was time. Suddenly, she felt furious. Furious that these men were strong and beautiful and stupid. Furious that it was all so unfair. Furious that she would never wake again on a soft valley dawn and watch the birds circle in the high morning air. Marto approached with his scythe, ready to harvest her blood. She tried to spit at him but her mouth was dry. The scythe sliced her throat and dark arterial fluid splashed onto the hard stone of the circle. The last thing she saw was yellow chaff mixing with her blood and draining over the edge.

The vital components that comprised her essence left her body without a backward glance and at once absorbed themselves into the fabric of the valley she loved.

Night fell and the strong and beautiful and stupid men walked back to the village.

Time To Kill

by
Janet

London Bridge Underground Station, late at night, is a bit scary. I found myself there after a business meeting. I felt very vulnerable and began to allow my imagination to play.

Eleven-ten pm is usually a good time to be here on the Underground. It's when the misfits are around. Or those people unaccustomed to being on the tube so late at night. You can tell them by their stance, their eyes, their demeanour. They keep their bags close to their bodies, their eyes downcast.

I'm here for the women. I like women, I always have. I like watching them, both overtly and covertly. I like to watch the way they move. I like to see how they're dressed. I stare. At my age, that's all I can do.

Click-clack, click-clack, one of my favourite sounds, delightful, familiar. A woman's high heels are tattooing on the hard floor. She's coming down the steps now – I won't look, not yet, and play my game. I think she'll be brunette, tall and be-suited.

I was wrong. She's small, very small and overweight. Not in a suit but a dress buttoned down the front, every fastening straining to hold her in. Her breasts are jiggling, wobbling. Even her feet are spilling over the confines of her shoes.

She's going to walk right in front of me now. Good, she noticed me. I saw her eyes flicker and quickly look away. She's trying to pretend she hasn't seen me but I know the signs. I know what to look for these days. Observation, that's the key. Observe your prey. It's what all hunters do.

The lining's coming down at the back of her jacket, she needs a stitch in that. This one has let herself go. Pity, she must have been a looker once.

Oh dear, she's moving to the nearest group of people, but they won't be able to help her, they're out of their minds, in completely different worlds. She's sitting down, putting her tatty briefcase on her lap. Oh, getting out a book. I wonder what it is. Wonder what her tastes are in reading? Nothing too high-brow I suspect.

That's right dearie, I'm still here. That glance spoke volumes. Know you've been picked out, don't you? Ooh, one of the drunks is lurching over to her.

She moves fast for a fat girl. Faster than I would have thought, straight towards me. Tut, tut, that briefcase wasn't closed. What a shame. Your own fault though. Full of mess, like the rest of you. That's right, cram everything in as quick as you can, you don't want to embarrass yourself even further.

Yes, I'm still watching you, intently. Every floppy move of your body. Racing away down the platform won't help you! Slow but sure, that's me.

The time indicator doesn't make the train come any quicker, however many times you feverishly look at it. She's behaving like a trapped animal. Perhaps she's been approached before. She looks the sort. I can almost smell her sweaty fear from here.

I always bring my green tartan bag on wheels with me. It confuses them. Wonder what she's doing out so late at night dressed for business. She doesn't look as though she could defend herself. She doesn't look – what's the word? Assertive, that's it.

That rabbit glance between me and the indicator board, as if anything is going to change, stupid girl. I wonder if she's noticed that she's the only woman on the platform? Eleven men and one oozing woman showing too much leg. Surely she knows that someone will approach her?

I can visibly see her trembling. What's she doing? Bending her chubby thighs, putting her briefcase on the ground. Oh, getting her book out again. Making sure she shuts the case, properly this time.

Correction on the indicator board. The train is going to Barnet and not to Golders Green. Wonder which one she's after? Archway girl possibly. Train approaching, just when she'd settled into the fantasy world of her paltry novelette.

Oh, a defiant glare. She's trying a bravery tack, striding piggishly away from me to the further carriage.

It always alarms them, the speed that a little old man with milky eyes and a green tartan bag-o-wheels can follow them.

That's right lady, sit down next to someone. Yes, you can give a sigh of relief; for a second. They never know that I'm right behind them. They always feel so safe when they reach their seat, especially when there are other people in the carriage. I can't avoid contact with your squelching thigh as it hangs over the edge of the seat. I'm brushing past you now girlie.

She's trying to withdraw inside herself, make herself smaller. Too much lard inside her for that. I'm going to sit diagonally across from you. She's pretending to disappear into her book again, but her little glances tell me the real story. This is my favourite time. I just stare.

Stare at her shoes that need polishing and reheeling. At her dress that has risen up and up, exposing her dimpled knees. It looks like they want to burst through her tights. A snag on the calf. Messy, very messy.

Now she's sat down her dress is gaping horribly, the buttons fighting to keep her decently covered. Glimpse of spilling breast. She's outgrown her jacket, looks like she'd been stuffed into it, like a sausage in skin-gut.

Porky face, beginnings of a double chin. Too much make-up, smudges of black under the eyes. Lipstick needs renewing, it's seeped into the crevices around her cracked lips. I wonder how old she is? That's something I like to pick up on straight away. Thirty-five? Yes, around thirty-five. No rings on her wedding finger.

Nice nails, long and painted at the end of her porcine digits. Yes, this one really has let herself go. Bet she drinks. Most of them do these days.

She's returning my stare! What's that look saying? She's scared and angry, all at the same time. Surely she's not trying to give me a warning? What could she possibly do to me? I'm an old man. A heart attack would just give me an easy way out.

She's trying to catch someone else's eye now. I don't think it matters who you look at my little puff-ball, no one here will understand your look. That's even if they bother to acknowledge it. The joy of my pursuits in London is that nobody cares enough to help or to intervene. I can do what I like. I've been doing this for twelve years. Each time being a little braver, a little more forthright, a little more outrageous. And even if the CCTV does pick me up, what would it see? Just a harmless old man, leaning on a sad battered shopping trolley.

My life only began when I started this. I've always been law abiding. A perfect grey citizen until I discovered how easy it is to frighten people. Brings surprising rewards. It's an aphrodisiac of power. It's about avoiding the social niceties. It's about behaving outside the norm. I wish I'd stumbled upon it earlier in life. How many people die without realising how easy it is to grasp power? I'm rambling now, is that age or acute pleasure? I need to concentrate on the girl.

Girl? By-blown woman would be more accurate. Is that a tiny line of sweat on her upper lip?

I'll try a smile. It's so satisfying. Smiles always have the same effect, it makes the fear in their eyes double. They never return my smiles. Funny that. It's my way of giving them a chance. But here's another girl that's failed.

Camden Town, a large exodus of bodies. She's really frightened now, her eyes are darting everywhere. She's standing up! She's not going to get off? No, she's moving seats! She's fighting back. That's rare, a little woman with a little power. Yes podgy, look back over your shoulder, my eyes will follow you before my body does. Settled now? Hope she doesn't move again, don't like too much exercise.

Does she really expect protection from that old drunk? Or the black woman buried in the corner? She does. Silly. Yes, I'm smiling at you porky! I'm coming closer and closer. No, don't gather yourself in, I'm not going to sit next to you, fool. I don't want your fat thighs rubbing against my flesh. I'm going to sit here, diagonally opposite you again. It's all part of the game. It's all meant to spook you and I can see it's working.

Kentish Town, the corner woman is getting off. What is fatty going to do now? Brave! Stay put and pretend to read your oh-so-interesting book and throw me the odd angry glare, are you? I'm still here, my eyes unwavering – just waiting for you to look up.

Not an Archway girl then. Or are you going way beyond your stop in the hope that I'll get off first?

It's you, me and the snoring drunk. I think it's time for the next step. I'm putting my hands on my knees, pushing them deliberately apart. I can see you watching me out of the corner of your eye. And what am I doing now girly? Slowly, slowly sliding my hands towards my crotch. It's an awfully long way to the next station, isn't it poppet?

Highgate, you're almost throwing yourself at the doors. Whimpering along the platform. You won't escape me. Run as fast as you like, I'll catch you eventually. That's it, rush off the platform, you may be out of sight but I can still hear your ragged breathing. I see you again, halfway up this long, long escalator. You're far too unfit to run up the whole way, aren't you? Highgate, longest escalators after Angel.

Perhaps this will serve as a warning to you to look after yourself in future.

You're out of my sight again, but I can hear your scuffy shoes scurrying toward the exit. I can hear you squeaking with fear, like a trapped animal. And in a way you are.

I'm cresting the escalator top now in my ludicrous bright red anorak. Clever, you've found someone on duty at this time of night. I see the man's face looking in disbelief at me.

What accusation are you jabbering? That I'm following you? That I'm harassing you? That I'm a potential rapist?

What do you think he sees? I'll tell you. He sees a bent, frail old man. He sees my bald head, my hooded eyes with the milky sheen of age, blinking slowly in the fluorescent lighting. My unwieldy green tartan shopping trolley on wheels, my bright red eye-catching jacket, my gnarled shaking hands. Watch as I give him a tired smile – see, he's responding; but to me, not to you! He thinks you're overreacting. He thinks you're just another sad spinster looking for attention.

I'm walking away from you, through the barrier. Ah, I have a choice, the main road exit or the Priory Gardens exit. Which one will I take? I think the Priory Gardens one, more options for where to go next. Bus to Muswell Hill or a hike to Crouch End. It's also the darkest entrance with trees and bushes and gardens.

I know your game, all the women do the same. You'll stay talking to the guard until you think I'm well gone. The guard will reassure you as best he can. Then you'll scuttle home, looking over your shoulder, terrified out of your wits. At my time of life, minutes, hours, become one. I can wait forever for that tingle of power. I savour the moments leading up to it and the days and weeks I can sustain it.

I don't have the power to hurt you physically. But I do have the power to terrify you. To be in your every waking thought. To make you dread looking out of your windows, or walk out of your front door. To hate travelling on the tube. To loathe exiting your workplace or lunching with friends, for fear of seeing a bright red anorak and tartan shopping trolley and my ever-watchful eyes.

You are another perfect victim. And I'm beyond the law. I never lay a finger on my ladies. I'm merely around. I never enter their property. I never speak to them directly. I'm just there, constantly, until I decide to move on.

Ah good, I chose the right exit. I can hear your single footsteps clattering up the stairs. The guard didn't believe your accusations after all. That's it, hurry home, past you go. I want to follow, not to lead.

In the still of the night, the wheels of the trolley have a really loud squeak, don't they, my chubby cherub?

Busy Guardian Angel

by
Andrew

It seems to me that no one has ever thought through the logistics of the whole Guardian Angel thing, so I thought I'd address the issue in the following story.

He didn't see the cyclist until it was too late. Not surprising really, the guy was speeding on the pavement and had no lights. Anyway, crash, and both of them were on the ground. Simon managed to pull himself up to a sitting position but there was a sharp pain in his back. He tried to stand, gave a little gasp and realised it would be impossible. The cyclist didn't seem very happy. Simon watched him get to his feet, swear a lot, most of it directed at him, get back on his bike and wobble off, still cursing stupid pedestrians.

Simon supposed he was in shock. He'd not been able to speak for a few moments, so hadn't even been able ask the angry cyclist to phone for help. This part of the road back from the station was pretty quiet at the best of times and now it was well past the last train time. He knew where his mobile was, sitting happily in his bedroom on charge, where he had foolishly left it this morning. He never forgot his mobile – it would be like forgetting your shoes. But forget it he had. He could see his breath in the freezing November air and suddenly began to feel afraid.

The path where he lay was several feet from the road and there were trees and bushes obscuring him. So when he heard the taxi, he didn't think it would be possible anyone would see him. He started to think of headlines about 'Man Frozen To Death Just Steps From Help'. He was surprised when the taxi halted and he heard someone get out and ask the driver to wait. And even more surprised when a rather portly middle-aged man arrived by his side, puffing heavily, although it was, as the headline had threatened, just steps away.

"Simon Clusky?" he heard the man ask.

"What?"

The man sighed. "Listen, I'm very busy. Are you Simon Clusky or not?"

"Yes, yes I am, but how do you… who do you… " Simon was still in shock.

"Right, I'll call you an ambulance. Otherwise, you'll freeze to death in five hours, twenty-two minutes and then my quotas will be all over the place."

"Quotas?"

But the man didn't reply and Simon watched him dial 999, give the exact location and hang up.

"About ten minutes they said." The portly man's mobile beeped with a text.

"What! That's miles away. Do they think I'm Superman or something? I'm getting too old for this."

"Too old for what?" Simon couldn't quite believe he was having this bizarre conversation late at night, with a strange man in the freezing cold, with him on the ground unable to move. He'd only had two drinks.

"Being a Guardian Angel. It's a young man's game."

"What? So are you saying you're my Guardian Angel?"

"Don't be ridiculous. No one gets their own. We're in the real world here. You wouldn't believe my caseload. Listen, I can't stand here all night chatting to you. I've got to be the other side of town before the night bus comes to run him over. You should be all right now. Just call out when the ambulance arrives or they'll never find you."

And with that the portly man was off, still puffing, back to the taxi.

The hospital released him the next morning. He'd bruised his vertebrae and his muscles had gone into spasm. As he walked home, his back felt stiff but gradually eased as he covered the two miles to his little house. Nearly home, he started to slow down. What was the hurry anyway? It wasn't as if he would be getting home to a house full of people who'd anxiously sit him down and give him tea and sympathy. In fact, the kindest words had been from his boss, who seemed to be more interested in when he would be back at work than enquiring about the state of his health.

Feeling a bit sorry for himself, Simon walked into a café. After all, he had nothing else to do on this unexpected day off. The smile from the pretty young girl at the counter fortified him and a few minutes later he was sitting in a cozy corner with a very large, very sweet hot chocolate. This was better. He felt his thoughts begin to wander. Who was that man last night? And what was all that stuff about Guardian Angels? Would he really have died if the portly man hadn't come along? In the warmth of the café, feeling better now, he could hardly believe it.

An hour later, he reached home. "Hello house," he always said when he got in. "Hello plant," he said to the big spider plant in the kitchen that seemed like it would live forever. He ruffled its leaves fondly. "I'm mad," he told himself. Well, at least this was one of the advantages of living alone, he thought. He made his way upstairs to find his pesky mobile and there it was. He picked it up and disconnected the charger, glancing at the small screen. No messages. What a surprise! Suddenly, it rang. He almost dropped it in shock. "Silly me," he thought. "It's probably someone calling to ask me if I'm OK." Although he couldn't imagine who, and he didn't recognise the number.

"Oh, hello Mr Clusky," said the voice. "Sorry, this is a bit embarrassing, but you'll remember me from last night…"

"Of course – my guardian angel – or, in fact, not mine but everybody's it seems."

Simon wouldn't forget that voice in a hurry. It was quite posh but with an accent he couldn't place.

"Listen, this is a wind-up, isn't it? Did you arrange to have me knocked over just so you could save me – and this is where you ask me for money?"

Simon wasn't born yesterday, but he did feel a bit bad about taking this tone with his – what should he call him – benefactor? After all, Simon thought, he may or may not have saved my life.

"No, I am very well compensated for my work, thank you. But I won't be if they find out that I forgot to hypnotise you after our little conversation. I've got a hypnotiser thing, which I'd left at home, just like you'd left your phone – and yes, before you ask I did know about that, we have extensive files. Anyway, it's too late to do you now. So basically, I could get into a lot of trouble with the people upstairs if you start going around saying that you were saved by an angel. Not that anyone would believe you, of course. But even so..."

Simon laughed. "I've got no one to tell. I don't think anybody would care anyway. So your secret's safe with me."

"Mr Clusky, that is so very understanding of you. When I realised my mistake, I was relieved to learn that I was dealing with a man of discretion. I re-read your file last night and I must say I am most terribly sorry to hear about your late wife and your struggles with depression. Although I was pleased to read that you're off the pills now."

He couldn't quite believe this conversation, but the man sounded genuine enough, and Simon felt a familiar ache in his heart. He tried not to think about his wife and her illness and her slow slipping away, and how he'd struggled to cope. In fact, it was only in the last few months he'd started to feel almost all right again.

"Yes, I am feeling better than I was this time last year." He had to enunciate the words carefully to get them up and over the lump in his throat.

"Well, Mr Clusky, I am most reassured by our conversation, and I must also apologise for being somewhat brusque last night, I'm normally far more..."

He heard the other man break off. "Oh, for goodness sake, another one already! I haven't even had my tea!"

"Sounds like they're keeping you busy anyway," Simon said.

"Yes, I know I shouldn't complain, but Novembers are always a bit of a rush and what with the other, er, angels, on holidays up you know where, we're quite shorthanded. Still, my own holiday is less than two hundred years away now, so it won't be long before I can have a good break myself. But in the meantime, duty calls."

Simon heard yet another text beep into the other man's phone and a gasp from his new – what should he call him? Not really friend, although he was starting to warm to this rather strange person.

"Gracious, I shan't get any sleep for another year at this rate," he heard the man mutter, and then, "Listen, I must go, and may I say I'm particularly pleased your name came to my phone last night and that I was able to help. Good afternoon, Mr Clusky."

"Hold on, just before you go, please." A crazy but rather exciting thought had arrived in Simon's head.

"Sounds like you're busy, and, well, one good turn deserves another, and all that… but I'm not doing anything right now, so if you wanted a hand with all this extra work you've got coming up…"

"Oh. Goodness. Well. That is most extraordinarily kind of you, Mr Clusky. And this is somewhat of an emergency, two cases coming up at the same time. That doesn't happen very often. And to be honest I'm not sure if I'll be able to make the lady and the train one. But I'll have to think about it. I need a quick confab with one of my colleagues who I can rely on to keep quiet. He had a similar dilemma recently, so he'll understand. One moment, I'll call you right back."

Simon ended the call and before one second had passed the phone was ringing again. It was, of course, the man.

"It's a yes, Mr Clusky. My colleague thinks it will be acceptable, just this once, and from having read your notes, I have sufficient faith in your good character to trust that you will not mention your task to the lady in question, nor indeed to anyone else."

"You have my word," replied Simon, feeling suddenly alive.

"Splendid! You'll have to leave right this second. Get a taxi to Elmsleigh station. The lady, red coat, black furry boots, woolly hat will be alighting the 14.46 from the city. It will be icy, she is going to slip and fall onto the tracks. All you have to do is rescue her, and of course, keep absolutely mum."

Thirty minutes later, a slightly breathless Simon was standing on the platform, nervously looking at his watch, hoping he would be up to the task. He looked at the rails. He supposed he could jump down easily enough; the electrics were overhead, so no danger there. Then he started to panic. What if it was a larger lady? Could he manage? But, he thought, it was the middle of the afternoon, there would surely be other people getting off the train, so he could always call for help.

He heard an engine noise and saw the 14.46 approach, just a small commuter train with four carriages. He positioned himself in the middle of the platform, waiting, nerves jangling.

The train came to a halt, the doors opened. No one got off! The doors beep-beeped and just before they closed a lady in a red coat, furry boots and woolly hat rushed out all in a fluster. She stood on the platform, rummaged in her bag as the train pulled away, looked at her phone and pressed a button to receive a call, at the same time walking briskly towards him with her head down.

"This must be it," Simon thought, "she'll slip on the ice while she's on the phone, and she's only a little thing. Not heavy at all. I can do this!" But to his surprise, the lady, still talking on the phone and looking distressed, hustled past him without slipping, indeed without noticing him at all, and headed for the bridge which connected the two platforms. Simon followed at a discreet distance. Maybe she slips on the other platform, he thought. But once he got down to platform level on the other side the indicator board caught his eye. He looked up. "Stand Back. The Next Train Does Not Stop At This Station."

What! He never mentioned this! Simon looked round in a panic to see where the red lady had gone. No sign of her at all! Then a little cry. He hadn't even seen her slip! He ran to the edge of the platform and there she was, lying awkwardly on the track, the contents of her handbag scattered everywhere, and her phone squawking uselessly some feet away. She looked up at him. He had only a second to see that she had lovely, lovely eyes.

The next moment, he was down on the track. "Soon get you up to safety," he mumbled. By this time the red lady was getting to her feet, although rather unsteadily. "My bag," she gasped. "No time for that," he puffed. And indeed there wasn't. He could hear the tracks beginning to sing with the sound of the Train That Does Not Stop At This Station.

He grabbed her roughly, not stopping to think where, and pushed her up onto the platform. She rolled somewhat ungraciously to safety along the concrete. Simon was still on the track. He looked for the oncoming train – there it was, still in the distance. It was going to be all right! He'd done it! He grabbed the platform edge and started to haul himself up. A great wave of pain shot through his back. He remembered with horror the muscle spasm from last night. He couldn't move, frozen and in agony. The train was much nearer now, going much faster than he could believe. He closed his eyes.

Suddenly, he sensed someone beside him, and felt himself being dragged to the other side of the tracks and pushed down onto the ground. A great rush of noise and air and the train was bowling past where he had been just a second before. Then a face leaning over him, looking at him with lovely, lovely eyes.

"Hello," she said. "We'd better move."

With difficulty she managed to help him back onto the platform and they staggered to a bench, his back still shouting at him. They flopped down, both breathing heavily. He looked at her the exact same moment she looked at him.

"Well," she said, "you must be my guardian angel or something, otherwise my silly little life would be over. Thank you. Thank you." She smiled the most wonderful smile, looked at him for a second, and began to sob uncontrollably. He put a comforting arm around her, wincing with pain. Thank you? But it was her who had had saved him! And when he realised that, he too started to cry.

They were still hugging and crying ten minutes later when the transport police found them, the train driver having reported people on the line. At the police station, they both had to give statements, and after a while the red lady's mother came to collect her daughter. Simon didn't have a chance to get her number and when the police finally released him she was gone. He walked home with a sense of deflation and disappointment.

"Hello house. Hello plant," he said sadly to his friends when he reached home. He sat in the kitchen staring at the wall for a few minutes, then sighed heavily. Life must go on, he supposed. As he finished that thought his phone rang.

"Oh Mr Clusky, are you all right?" asked the angel.

"I'll recover," muttered Simon.

"I'm having to apologise to you once again. But very good news. It's always extremely lucky when you get a double guardian reverse turnaround situation – they only happen very rarely. And your good luck starts in twelve seconds. You won't be hearing from me again – not that you'll need to, of course. But I couldn't have wished it to happen to a nicer man. Cheerio, thank you, and all the very best for your wedding."

The phone went dead as the doorbell chimed. A very confused Simon eased himself and his bad back to the door. Standing there was the red lady with her lovely, lovely eyes, some flowers and a bottle of what looked like champagne.

"Simon… sorry to bother you. But I heard you say your address when you were giving your statement. And I thought, well, one good deed deserves another. And this seems strange, but I think we've… we've made a connection…" She looked at him shyly.

"Come in," said Simon, suddenly feeling light and warm. "Let me find my best champagne glasses and we'll make a toast to guardian angels." And with that, he ushered her in, closed the door and left his old life behind.

Plane Speaking

by
Janet

I had a genuine out of body experience whilst volunteering for retrogressive hypnosis. I saw myself drift out of my body through my head and float up to the ceiling so that my 'spirit eyes' were looking down on my physical feet. It was a really strange sensation. I was then overcome with fear that I wouldn't be able to slide back into myself. That was the seed for this story.

My barrister has told me I'm not eliciting enough sympathy. Apparently, the jury don't warm to me.

I'm a schoolteacher by profession. I've never enjoyed it, teaching, but at the time of choices – you know, thirteen – I couldn't think of anything else. I chose art, a foolish choice really. Art without passion, well it's an anomaly. Consequently, I'm less than adequate.

Because of this, although I've taught for twenty years, I never have, nor ever will reach the heights of Head of Department. I don't even physically fit the department. I have no flamboyance in my personal style, and no flair for dress or colour. Understandably, I suppose, I do not gel with the other teachers. I do have an ability to be objective, so I can stand quite easily on the outside and see all this. And, of course, when I choose to project myself, I have the added advantage – although advantage is perhaps an inappropriate word – of being able to be right in the centre of their bitchy conversations about me.

Now their conversations about me are conducted in shocked hurried whispers; their words mumbled behind upheld hands, mouths murmuring close to earlobes.

I married when I was twenty-six. A solid, sensible marriage, a blanket. Graham and I rub… rubbed along pretty well in a companionable sort of way.

Sex was never high on my list of priorities, although Graham seemed to have quite an appetite for it. My experiences before Graham were quite limited. A few fumblings at the back of the cinema, snogging against the brick wall of the youth club, hands on my breast at the bus stop. The usual sort of thing, I suppose.

I recall that Graham was delighted at my virginal state. He didn't wait until the wedding night to rob me of it. I found the experience painful and absurd. Between you and me, I thought the whole of it, the whole sexual act, was like some obscure joke. But that's when I first discovered I had the gift. Again, a strange word, gift. Gift implies it is a desired treasure, like being born with perfect pitch or an IQ that is stunningly high. You see, they place you on the outside of everything, special gifts. And once there, they cannot be smashed or returned. They are more an affliction, a burden. But as I just said, it was when I was having my first sex that I discovered mine. I found the procedure so repugnant that I propelled myself up and away from the lumpy naked bodies on our bed and took flight.

The first few times I was worried in case I didn't return at a suitable time, but my body-mind would call me as the last groan and shudder would be erupting from Graham's being.

I bore him two children – two girls, Megan and Stephanie. Parenting merely compounded my feelings of ineptitude. As a voracious mouth would clamp onto my sore split nipple, I would eject myself away. Far away. Astral planeing became my saviour.

Graham thought, and I never dissuaded him of his belief, that I loved the process of breast-feeding. He said he loved to watch me as I would slip into a deep state of tranquility before his very eyes. From the ceiling, I would watch him gazing at me and the child adoringly. I did suffer guilt, but what could I do?

My barrister – I didn't tell you his name, how rude of me – John Bracken, his name is John Bracken. He says I have a cold detached air and according to him it's off-putting, even scary. He doesn't, well can't understand – just like Graham really – that in the courtroom I am detached, I'm literally not there inside my physical self. I'm off flying, escaping the monotony of court procedure. This morning I was at the graveside with weeping relatives. When and if I am in court, the jury's decision is of no consequence, whatever it is.

Until I began breastfeeding, I'd always astrally projected the same way. From a horizontal position, my body always eased itself out through the top of my head, feet last. I would then float gently until my spirit rested it's back against the ceiling, almost as though checking the position of my physical body before streaming away.

But when I projected from the enforced sitting position for breast-feeding, I made a surprising discovery. I could see right through into the top of my head. I mean straight through into my brain, into its actual cavities. Actually, see the demons plotting within.

At first it was just that, a discovery.

But then there came a time when the demons began to talk to me. At first, I had control of them, not anymore. I used to be able to switch them off by simply slipping back into my body, but they got wise. They began to prevent me coming back into myself unless I promised to do their bidding. It's a fearful sensation floating in limbo, being able to touch yourself without being able to climb into yourself and breathe life back into your body. I suppose if I'd been stronger – but then, I'm not, am I?

The initial tasks the demons asked me to perform were childlike, silly; almost as though they were testing me. Burn the supper, run a cold, rather than a hot bath for the girls. The silliness, though aggravating, was manageable. Graham merely teased me, told me I was going dotty at an early age.

That phase lasted years. But then, quite suddenly, the demons began to demand more control of me. They began violently ejecting me from myself, sending me hurtling unexpectedly into the atmosphere. It was disorientating, terrifying. They would leave me suspended on the ceiling whilst they stared up at me, laughing.

When the demons allowed me back, sometimes whole agonising hours would have elapsed. A screaming pain would pulse in my head and a high-pitched whine would whirl around and around until exhaustion overcame me.

Graham insisted on a doctor's visit. The migraine pills were, as I knew they would be, completely useless.

I fought with them. I remember fighting, saying no, begging them to leave me be. They merely stepped up their campaign of indiscriminate ejection. It took the demons less than two months before I gave myself over to them.

My new tasks began to take on humiliating agendas. Wetting the bed, that was one of the first. A grown woman, wetting the bed. At the start, Graham was sympathetic, but eventually made up the bed in the spare room with a plastic sheet for me until we were 'able to sort out the cause'. He also sought out some counselling numbers as he thought I should explore the problem. What was the point? I knew. I also knew the demons would never allow me to share them with anyone else.

Other humiliating tasks were demanded of me. I wasn't allowed to wash my hair for days on end until the Headmaster was compelled to have a quiet word with me. I was forced to dress in outlandish clothes and make-up to draw embarrassing comments to myself.

I fought with them only once more, when they plotted the murders. I became frantic, trying to stop myself astral planeing, but it was useless. By this time I was their puppet, their plaything. They could throw me out of myself at will.

It's funny, placing me in a cell, in custody, in isolation. I'm a prisoner at risk due to the apparent atrocities of my killings. But, of course, I'm not confined at all. No, not at all. Last night, I was at John Bracken's house. He was laughing all evening. He's such a sober man, I was surprised. He was playing host at his own dinner party. He eats with his mouth open, I wouldn't have thought he would do that.

The removal to the spare bedroom, I realised in retrospect, was part of a master plan for they began to ask me to gather things and hide them in the room. Strange things, a bradawl, sugar, a star-shaped cake mould, a bread knife. I did their bidding as I assumed these things were harmless enough.

They told me precisely to the minute a week before. I know the information affected me, Graham kept gently asking me if there was anything wrong. What could I say?

Three Thursdays from now, precisely, my demons have informed me when and how I will be taking my life for their gratification.

The three of them share equal power. They always give their commands in unison. I should explain they don't actually speak, they project their thoughts like arrows into my consciousness, but obviously they can only do this when I'm out of body. They never do it when I'm at home, so's to speak.

On the actual night, I laced the stew with my sleeping pills that I'd long had on prescription. I was told to crush my tranquillizers into the custard of the trifle and add extra sugar. We ate as a family, as usual.

I turned up the fire in the lounge, complaining of the cold, just as I'd been instructed. They were asleep by nine. I went upstairs and collected my magpie selection of goods.

Holding your child's heart in your hands is the worst agony. And the hacking sounds of wrenching it away from the other organs – I thought my tears would never cease. As I murdered each of my loved ones, and not one of them cried out, I followed the plan, squeezing their hearts into the star moulds and covering them with sugar that turned crimson in an instant. It took me four hours to kill them and arrange them as the demons wished.

Then, as instructed, I left the front door ajar and telephoned the police. I wasn't allowed to change or clean myself. When they arrived I was sat, as told, in the triangle between the bodies, their hearts placed in their starry moulds upon their foreheads, with the bradawl in my left hand and the bread knife in my right.

Cat Fright

by
Andrew

You never quite know what's going on with cats, do you?

It was cold, dark and late. Drink had been taken and steps were unsteady. Samuel had enjoyed a good night with his old mate Pete, but instead of being pleasantly squiffed and thinking of nonsense, he was worrying about the guinea pig.

It belonged to the son of his girlfriend Marjorie. Marjorie was no animal lover. He wished she was. How could you not like animals? Marjorie had a young son and last year, worried that the boy needed something to love and had no proper father, she bought him a guinea pig. After a brief period of excitement, however, the creature had been abandoned like a useless toy, hidden away in a spare room on rodent death row. Sometimes, Samuel and Marjorie would argue.

"You take it then!" Marjorie would fling at him.

He knew he should. He'd seen guinea pigs in a big cage in the park, lots of them living together, squeaking and jumping and sniffing and fucking. That would be the life for the guinea pig of Marjorie's son he thought. The poor thing didn't even have a proper name. The guinea pig of Marjorie's son was the best they could do. But Samuel couldn't take it in. He had a busy life, and anyway when they suggested it to her boy one day, he threw himself into a rage and said he loved it and wanted it and would look after it forever and ever, and it would never die, and it was his pet, and his and his and his.

But just two mornings ago, on a whim, as he was leaving Marjorie's house after his usual Sunday night sleepover, he sneaked the rodent - cage, rank straw and all - into his car and took it home. Neither Marjorie nor Marjorie's son had as yet noticed the disappearance of the guinea pig of Marjorie's son. The creature now lived in his utility room with fresh straw and water and small slices of apple. He resolved to bring it to the park at the weekend to see if they could take the poor thing in and give it one last chance of squeaking and fucking before its tiny life was over.

He would call Marjorie in a minute for their goodnight call, he thought. Not that he had anything much to say anymore. Unless she had noticed the missing creature, in which case a major row would be brewing. Talking to M every night had become a routine after nearly five years and if that routine was broken, something between them would be broken too. After the call, he would curl up in bed with himself and a crisp, fat, new book. Then he would listen to the icy waters of the shipping forecast and drift into the easy sleep of landlubbers.

Nearly home.

A movement caught his eye. Fox? But a tiny trace of meow reached his ears. He walked back. Peering into a garden, he saw a glimpse of blackness shadowing behind the bin. He kneeled down and did the automatic kissing noises he always made whenever he saw a cat. He'd loved cats ever since he'd had one aged five. It had helped to take his mind off the rows in the house and the occasional crash of breaking crockery. He would calm the nervy cat – a taken in stray – hold it tight and reassure it and him that everything would be all right. He missed that cat even now, even more than his dead parents. One day, when life was more settled, he would take in a new cat from a cat's home and love it like he had before.

He'd been crouched there by the bin for a while now making puss puss noises. Then a tiny splash of pink tongue helped him make out the form of a small black cat; not a kitten, but young and thin, looking like it would break a heart.

"Here baby, come on, puss puss." The cat took nervy steps towards him. It was such a pretty little thing. Short haired and black as the hills. Samuel was nothing if not a seducer, although it had been a while since he had seduced anything. "Come on beauty," he whispered. The cat nearly made it to his outstretched fingers when a motorbike went by at speed. The cat freaked and disappeared behind the bin. Samuel tried for another minute or two. Then it started to rain. Cursing, but not defeated, he made for home. There was some tuna in the fridge, a bit of cheese too. This was no night for a little cat to be out. He would do the right thing as a human and see if he could coax the animal from under the bin and into the warmth of his cosy house with its slumbering wood burning stove.

Five minutes later, he returned with a bowl of food, intent on his saintly task. St Francis of Streatham, his ego reassured him softly. But there was no sign of the little cat. He waited for several minutes, gently calling and caressing until the lights went on in the house and he beat an embarrassed middle class retreat. Feeling unexpectedly empty, he returned home and called Marjorie. He considered telling her about the void in his heart but realised it was inappropriate. Wasn't it Marjorie's job to fill that space?

As Marjorie complained about her sister, Samuel fantasised about their arrangement. When he was with her, he lived in a bowl of peaches and cream with just a bit too much sugar. Marjorie had soft hairless olive skin that he loved to endlessly stroke: her arms, her elbows, between her legs. He loved to sniff her all over, she was clean and full with high-end product, smelling of a summer's day, or a Japanese bathhouse, or a honey scented rose garden. It aroused him to inhale her deeply as she dozed, bringing his nose close to her skin and losing himself in those soft laureth tones. He would press gently on her thighs and wonder, amazed at how the flesh would spring back like a mini trampoline. If she woke and caught him red-handed at his devotions, she would push him away in disgust. Later, unable to sleep, he would secretly pull away the covers to simply gaze upon her fruity form. Sometimes, they would have a sort of sex, they would fondle and he would grab at the tub of moisture she allowed him to keep by her bed, apply two coats, and ease himself into the cool clean space he found there until he liberated the stresses of the day.

The next night he looked for the little cat, but no sign. The day after that it snowed. Coming home sober mid-evening he looked again in vain. He was almost at his house when he saw a woman – maybe a girl - standing lost near his house. His interest piqued, he slowed to take her in. Black as the hills, bare legs, in an old raincoat, wellington boots and a thin flowery dress.

"You OK, love?"

"Cold."

"You need to get in the warm."

"Suppose."

He couldn't quite place the accent. London, but with something underneath.

"Can I call you a taxi or something?"

"Neow, it's all right."

"Honey, you're going to freeze here. Can't I just walk you home?"

"I'm fine." But she looked sad and pathetic. He hadn't called Marjorie yet, but he made a decision.

"Listen, if you got nowhere to go, you can stay at my house. Just for tonight," he added, he didn't want some random heroin addict moving in.

"Don't worry 'bout me, I been outside before."

She caught his eye, just for a second. He detected uncertainty there, a sort of push and pull. Maybe he could reel this one in. Jesus, what was he thinking?

"Hey, why don't you just come in for a cuppa and warm yourself for ten minutes. No funny business, promise."

She didn't answer, but just stood there in the snow looking vulnerable. His heart went out to her, what kind of shit was she going through? Although he couldn't deny a sexual pull either.

"OK. Well, I hope you get somewhere safe soon. If you change your mind, I'm at 72, just up there."

She nodded and wrapped the coat around her tighter.

Moments later he was at his front door and just as he was about to close it, he saw her outside.

"Got any milk?"

"Err... sure. Come in."

Feeling slightly charged by the risk he was taking, he ushered her in, sat her down on the sofa and threw a log onto the woodburner, which responded by bursting into life.

"So, shall I make you a nice hot milky cuppa?"

"No, just milk," she said softly.

"OK, milk it is. Sure you don't want anything warm, like a hot chocolate, or a brandy?"

"No, just milk."

In the kitchen, he made a tea for himself and when he returned with her milk, he saw that she had taken off her wellies and coat and was sitting on the sofa's edge, looking around nervously.

"Here you go."

She took the milk and he positioned himself at the other end of the sofa, furthest away from the door. Let me give her an escape, he thought. Indeed, she looked as if she was about to run. She sniffed the milk cautiously, then took a tiny sip.

"Ummm," she mumbled, then drank the whole glass in one go. She wiped her mouth with her bare forearm, then rubbed the same arm onto her leg. A tiny drop of milk remained there, just above her knee. He had a sudden urge to lick it off the shiny dark skin. But he'd promised no funny business, and whichever way you looked at it, doing that would be funny. She saw him staring and without pause raised her leg and licked the milky spot clean.

"God, you're flexible," he said, masking his shock. As she'd raised her leg, he'd seen right up into the knickerless space between her thighs.

"Are you a dancer or something?"

She looked confused by the question. Immediately he regretted it.

"Sorry, didn't mean to pry."

He sipped his tea and looked at her. Not much fat but enough to get hold of. Black skin so shiny he could almost see his face in it. Slightly pointy nose, but on her it worked just fine. And odd hair, short, straight and almost downy. Not

Afro hair. He wanted to ask about her heritage but stopped himself. It was a crass question under any circumstances. And besides, now she was settling more onto the sofa, curling herself into its contours and at the same time moving closer.

"You look a bit more comfortable now. Must be something in the milk."

She moved from her curled position and leaned towards him.

"I like milk."

Jesus, I've got a weird one here, he thought. Without pause she put one hand on his thigh, then the other, and began moving her hands on and off, up and down. Samuel got an immediate erection, a first class A1 type he'd not had in years.

She leaned against him, still pressing up and down on his thigh, and placed her head under his neck. He felt a sandpapery sensation by his jugular and realised she was licking him. It was unnerving, sensual and smelt not unpleasantly of warm spit. He stroked her slightly oily hair and then down her back, inside her dress where the zip was broken.

"Umm," she said and stopped licking. Very turned on, he kept stroking and tried to angle himself to bring fuller body contact. But to his disappointment, when he looked into her face, he saw that her eyes were nearly closed, just slits, and her breathing was regular but oddly grumbly. Poor thing, he thought, she must have bronchitis from being out in the cold all that time. Feeling slightly ashamed of himself and his base urges, he moved them both into a more comfortable position where he could relax. His erection lingered a few moments but soon expired and drifted away to hard-on heaven, where he imagined it frolicking with past hard-ons like the guinea pigs in the park.

The girl was fully asleep now. Her body felt light and comfortable against his, and seemed to be pumping out lots of heat. He felt more relaxed than he'd been in ages. His mind wandered into a soon to sleep state. He thought of his parents and their angry lives and inexplicably a well of forgiveness rose in his heart. His last thought before he slept was that they did their best.

The buzzing of his mobile woke both of them. The girl was no longer lying on him, it looked like she'd been sleeping in front of the woodburner, but now she was standing, with a startled look on her face.

"Hey, easy there, just the phone, no problem."

His words seemed to calm her but didn't stop her from pulling her wellingtons back on and reaching for her coat. He looked at his phone. 07.18 and six missed calls from Marjorie. For some reason the information didn't send him into a panic as it might have done in the past. The girl was at the living room door now.

"You don't have to go just yet," he said. "Stay and have a bit of breakfast."

"Already had some," she replied.

"You've had some?"

"Gotta go," said the girl, and before he could stop her she was out in the hallway, opening his front door.

"Wait," he cried, but she didn't.

She ran down his path, coat flapping, not looking back; then vanished around the corner. He stood for a few seconds in the cold air, then smiled to himself. Feeling unexpectedly good, he walked whistling back into the hallway but then stopped. Some of the doors inside were wide open. He always closed the inside doors when he went out in case of fire.

"Fuck," he said to himself. Running upstairs he found his bedroom door wide open too. She must have sneaked about while I was asleep, he thought. But his visible loose coins and notes were still there on his bedside table, so was his iPod and the Euros he kept under the Buddha paperweight. Weird. Maybe she was just curious, he thought.

Alarm over, his good mood returned. He made a coffee, a proper one this time from his espresso machine; why not pamper myself, he thought. He was always in a rush, what for? And Marjorie. Why was he still with her when he didn't love her? What was the point? He would end it gently but firmly, he resolved. There must be someone out there who could love and be loved back. It was as if the morning had opened all sorts of new possibilities. Savouring the rest of his coffee, he had a leisurely shower and put on his best suit for work. He added the yellow pocket-handkerchief that looked good in the mirror, but he'd never had the courage to wear. Today, he didn't care what people thought. He decided to speak to his boss too - about that transfer. Definitely!

Just one more thing to do before he left the house. Humming a jaunty pop tune from the nineties he chopped up some apple and added raisins and a bit of cucumber. He'll enjoy this, he thought fondly. But when he went into the utility room, he stopped short. The door to the cage was wide open and straw was scattered over the floor. Suddenly, feeling freaked, he reached inside the cage and searched it thoroughly. All that remained of the guinea pig of Marjorie's son was a speck of blood, some bits of fur and a tiny little rodent ear.

Mild Rebellion

By
Janet

My Gran was the sweetest, gentlest woman in the world. We were horrified when she was moved by the council to a place where she was bullied by her new neighbour. We were able to move her elsewhere. But it made me think, what would it be like if you were bullied by a family member?

'Mutton dressed as lamb, that's what you'll look like!' Violet said sharply.

Maude edged up to the glass door and peered in, but her breath caused the window to steam up, rendering the exercise futile. She hesitated and made the slightest move to leave when suddenly the door was wrenched open.

'Is it stuck again? It's a real pig this door sometimes!'

'I knew you wouldn't be able to go through with it!' Violet snapped.

It was just the spur that Maude needed and she staunchly followed the young girl inside.

'What can I do to help you Madam?'

'Ah, well...' Maude faltered as she suddenly noticed an oddity about the girl's ears. The top half were pierced through and held about twenty gold hoops. She was bought sharply back to reality.

'Have you got an appointment?'

An easy one: 'No.'

'What did I tell you?' Violet butted in. 'You'll never get in without an appointment. You never listen.'

'We're not busy, might be able to fit you in now?'

'That would be splendid, if you can.'

'What do you want, cut and blow-dry?' the girl asked.

'Blow-dry?' Maude queried.

'If you're foolish enough to stay for goodness sake, don't go for anything fancy!' Violet warned, 'You'll only regret it.'

'Actually I'd like a cut, colour and a blow-dry.' There, it was said.

'For heaven's sake, how much do you think that little lot will cost?'

The spikey-haired girl yelled: 'Patrick!' and began to walk away from the reception area, her ripped jeans gaping with each step.

A handsome man bounded out from the back of the salon, flicking long dark ringlets over his shoulder as he approached.

'Yes Sandra?'

'What a lovely voice,' thought Maude.

'This lady would like a cut, colour and blow-dry.'

Patrick turned dazzling blue eyes towards her.

'No fool like an old fool, that's what he's thinking,' muttered Violet.

'If I start you now, I'll be able to squeeze you in before my next customer.'

Shrugging off her coat, Maude felt decidedly frumpy. She was relieved when a dramatic gown in navy blue and red was slipped around her shoulders. She was led to a soft leather chair where Patrick began without preamble to run his fingers through her hair.

'What did you have in mind?'

Maude felt an instantaneous tightening in her chest. She frantically searched for Violet, who had taken this moment to desert her. Before Maude's panic escalated Patrick's soothing voice cut in.

'If you're not too sure, may I make a suggestion?' Thankfully, not waiting for her reply, he swept on. 'Your hair is very fine, we need a cut to give it a little more body. I suggest we follow the natural wave of the hair but tuck it right into the nape of the neck here? Then feather these sides so that they softly fall onto the cheeks.'

Maude could hardly believe he was talking about her hair, he was making everything sound like a painting.

'Feathered onto your cheeks?' Violet was back. 'Tell him you want it tucked behind your ears, like you always have it.'

'Yes, that sounds lovely.'

'Now colour,' Patrick said. 'We'll have to be careful with your hair being so fine. We don't want the colour to look too strident. Petra,' he called, 'colour charts please. Have you had your hair dyed before?'

'Not really.'

'You either have or you haven't,' Violet barked.

'Actually no, never.'

'Right. What sort of colour do you fancy?' He asked as a chubby young girl handed him a chart of pastel hair shades.

'It's a little confusing, isn't it? Not the pink, or the blue. Do you think the lavender would suit me?'

'Yes, I think it would.' Patrick gave Petra a nod and she walked away purposefully.

'Lavender? You're plain old Maude, not the Queen of Sheba!' Violet spat with a snort of derision.

Maude tried to ignore her.

'We'll do the colour first,' Patrick said, as he began to place a plastic cape on her shoulders. Petra reappeared, wheeling a small trolley and placed it on Patrick's right side. He began to paint each tress of Maude's hair in a deep, vibrant damson.

Violet choked on a cackle of laughter. 'You'll be frightening young children!'

A tremor of apprehension led Maude to give voice to her fears.

'It won't be this bright in the end will it?'

'No, no,' said Patrick with a chuckle. 'It's always deceptive, what goes on and what it ends up like are very different.'

Not a totally reassuring reply. The last piece of hair painted, Patrick smiled, set a timer on the counter in front of her and whisked away. In seconds, Sandra was there giving her a pile of magazines and asking, 'Tea or coffee?'

'Tea please, milk, two sugars.'

'If you won't think of your waistline at least think of your heart,' Violet said.

A sudden picture sprung into her mind of Violet's dumpy figure at the scratched kitchen table, ladling honey onto a piece of toast for herself, the hard lines of her face etched deeper by the cold fluorescent lighting.

'Won't be a minute,' chirruped Sandra, causing the unpleasant image to disappear.

Maude allowed herself to take in her surroundings. She was surprised to see men having their hair done. One girl, she assumed it was a girl, appeared to be having the sides of her hair shaved off completely. She contented herself by reading her magazines. And before she knew it, the timer jangled its warning to Patrick that twenty minutes had passed. He checked her hair and called: 'Petra, wash off please.'

Maude was escorted to a row of basins. But here she had to sit down and tip her head backwards, as opposed to forwards over the bath, the standard procedure that Violet had employed. Instead of the usual, 'Family Shampoo – Large', she found herself having to make a choice between three beautiful natural fruit flavours. And on top of this, she was invited to choose a conditioner, a product she only knew through television adverts. The whole hair-washing experience was a pleasure; the girl gently massaging her scalp, easing away unnecessary tensions.

With towel-turbaned hair Maude was returned to her leather throne. Patrick removed the towel and humming softly, began combing the wet tangles gently, without making Maude wince once. Patrick produced a pair of scissors, then horror of horrors, as he began to cut he began to talk. He was expecting to have a conversation with her!

'What made you decide to have your hair dyed?'

'Stupidity?' Violet snorted.

'I just felt, well, in need of a change.'

'In need of a change at sixty-eight?' her sister whipped in.

'That's as good a reason as any,' Patrick said.

But not the truth, thought Maude.

'Don't Maude.' An unexpected plaintive note was in Violet's voice.

Maude immediately closed the door on her thoughts.

Reassured, Violet's voice took on its usual edge.

'He doesn't want to hear your drivel anyway!'

Maude trembled imperceptibly. Violet always controlled her and seemingly always would. The hopelessness of her situation caused a tear to trickle forlornly down Maude's cheek.

Patrick was watching her intently in the mirror. Caught out, Maude tried to explain.

'Sorry, my sister Violet died recently, well, just a fortnight ago actually. I was just thinking about her.'

'I see, I'm sorry,' he said.

'We shared a house together. I'm used to her being around. She's always done my hair for me before.'

'Really?' It was never his policy to criticise someone else's work. 'And did you do her hair in return?'

'Oh no, no, she would never have trusted me with a pair of scissors, cack-handed she called me. Violet always went to the hairdressers,' Maude said, a wan smile hovering on her face. 'And she said I had two left feet.'

A vision of her sister leapt into her mind. Violet, just about to leave the house, her stocky figure in a royal blue coat, her newly permed hair covered by a colourful head-square, turning and sneering at her, 'You, at a tea dance? You're not going to make me a laughing stock.' And the front door slamming shut.

'And do you have two left feet?' Patrick smiled.

'To be honest, I've never had the chance to put them to the test,' Maude whispered.

Patrick chuckled and pointed out that now she had an ideal opportunity to try, there was no one to stop her. He was right in a way, there wasn't anybody physically stopping her anymore.

'Actually, visiting a hairdresser and having my hair dyed is a little bit of a rebellion,' Maude confided.

'Really?' And what's your next wicked step going to be?'

'A tea dance!' Maude was surprised to hear herself say.

'And where will your tea dance be?

'Oh, the Ritz, of course!'

Patrick laughed as he repeated: 'Of course!'

Maude realised that she was the cause of his pleasure. She who never made jokes or witty conversation.

It was too much for Violet.

'Shut up, you're making a spectacle of yourself! Anyway, you'd only be lonely at a tea dance. You've never been able to make friends.'

Maude shuddered.

'Alright?' Patrick queried.

'Sorry, yes, fine, fine.' But Maude fell silent.

His warm voice broke into her reverie, 'I expect you miss her?'

'Yes, she was a very strong personality.'

'She sounds it.'

His words acted as a trigger. She felt a heat sweeping through her limbs – she only realised it was anger when 'I hated her!' burst from her lips. She began to tremble.

'I'm sorry,' Patrick said startled.

Maude felt compelled to explain.

'It's just that she could manipulate me so well, she used to make me so angry and I couldn't retaliate. She had a bad heart, you see. I used to feel so helpless against her. She died of a heart attack in the end.'

'How upsetting for you.'

'Yes.' Maude was glad her thoughts were private from all but Violet as an unbidden snatch of her sister's death replayed itself.

Maude had brought home some Cruise brochures from the travel agents. It was a secret desire she had nursed for years. The idea of floating on a moving island and the merciful silence she imagined it would bring. Her sister began with her usual sarcasm.

'Do you think money grows on trees? Do you know how expensive cruises are? Or did you just not think about the cost? You don't think about much really, do you? Do you? Lady Muck swanning off around the world, you couldn't find your way to the corner shop, so how you think you'll find Dover.'

'They go from Felixstowe too.' It was a statement of fact, not a criticism, but it inflamed Violet, who became angrier and angrier, her insults escalating in volume and viperishness. Spittle began to form at the corners of her mouth. Maude watched her sister with detached fascination.

She watched as Violet suddenly clutched at her chest and stopped speaking mid-barb, her mouth held open in a silent agony. With eyes popped wide, one hand started to claw towards her, presumably for help, before her stocky body slumped unceremoniously onto the kitchen floor, catching the table with her right temple on the way down. Maude watched her sister twitch, three, four times and then there was peace and stillness.

Maude, outwardly calm apart from a tremble in her hands and an unnatural slowness in her movement, stepped around Violet and made herself a cup of tea. She then sat at the opposite end of the kitchen table, slowly sipping her tea and staring at the lumpy body of her sister, before eventually getting up and ringing the doctor.

'Yes,' Maude said softly, 'I was there when it happened.'

Maude tensed, but Violet was nowhere to be heard.

She suddenly caught sight of herself in the mirror and smiled as she acknowledged the ridiculousness of the situation. Here she was, a foolish old woman with sopping wet hair festooned in a gaudy colour, discussing her sister's death, much as she would discuss the weather.

'Sorry, I'm quite sure you don't want to hear about such a depressing topic!'

'You'd be surprised what people discuss with their hairdressers!' Patrick said lightly.

Maude responded warmly and all too soon their gentle banter came to an end as Patrick held a mirror at the back of her head, so she could see the overall effect of his artistry. Maude was delighted, the colour and cut made her feel younger and cheekier.

'Thank you,' she murmured.

'Anytime,' he replied with a mock bow. As he led her to reception, he said: 'You'll need a trim in about six weeks, so I'll see you again then.'

Maude liked the fact it was an order and not a question.

'Great. Do you like it?' Sandra inquired.

'Yes, yes, very much.' Maude was a little taken aback at the bill, but happily paid it before making her way to the coat-hooks. A new coat next, in pink, she thought as she began to struggle into her mac.

"Allow me,' a rich dark voice commanded.

'Oh,' Maude turned and saw a man of about her age, beaming at her.

'Well, thank you,' Maude flustered. 'If you don't mind.'

'What man minds helping an attractive woman?'

Attractive woman, thought Maude.

'Why, thank you kind Sir,' she managed to say, before blushing furiously and lowering her eyes.

'Anytime,' he replied, 'Goodbye.'

'Goodbye,' Maude called cheerily to him as she strode confidently towards the exit. And as she pulled the door to a close she whispered, 'And goodbye to you too Violet. Forever.'

Look At The Tits On That

by
Andrew

Men! Come on, don't deny it. You've looked at women this way,
haven't you? Oh yes.

'Look at the tits on that,' said the man.
'Yeah,' agreed the other.

'Fucking massive,' exclaimed the man.
'Huge,' concurred the other.

'And look at that arse,' observed the man.
'Nice,' added the other.

'You couldn't get a fag paper between those
    cheeks,' theorised the man.
'No way,' mumbled the other.

'Fucking slags though,' muttered the man.
'Both of 'em,' ventured the other.

'Bitches,' spat the man.
'Whores,' declaimed the other.

'Where have all the nice men gone,' said the
    woman.
'No clue,' replied the other.

'Not seen anyone I've fancied for ages,'
    exclaimed the woman,
'Me neither,' agreed the other.

'I mean look at the men in here,' observed
　　the woman,
'Rather not,' giggled the other.

'Those two over there, for example,"
　　gestured the woman.
'The nasty looking ones?' questioned the
　　other.

'Look at that big belly,' noted the woman,
'And the sneery face,' stated the other.

'Wouldn't touch them with a bargepole,'
　　snorted the woman,
'No way,' retorted the other.

'Hahahahaha,' laughed the woman,
'Hehehehehe,' added the other.

'Lets' go to the Dog and Duck,' suggested
　　the woman,
'Nicer men in there,' opined the other.

'Best get home to the missus,' sighed
　　the man.
'Me too,' said the other.

Dalai Lama

by
Janet

The Tube, such a playground for madness.

'Dalai Lama, Dalai Lama?' questioned the man opposite me. 'Oh yes, Dalai Lama, the gentleman made into a religious icon by mankind? Yes, I remember him, short chap, great friends with Barbara Windsor from the *Carry On* films.' He paused, flicking imaginary dust off his grubby jeans, meticulously turned up to rest mid-calf. 'Oh yes, she did very well for herself, bit too busty for me and a bit too short.'

I noticed his plimsoll lace was undone. 'No, no I don't know what became of her, probably died in drunken obscurity, most of them do.' He listened momentarily. 'Film stars,' he explained. He crossed one leg over the other extravagantly and shifted in his seat.

Whoever was speaking to him was obviously very engaging although difficult to place as the man's eyes fidgeted to the roof, the door to his right, the window opposite, in fact anywhere where they did not light upon other eyes. He suddenly began to chuckle; deep, resonant, rich, brimful of warmth. 'Couldn't take her with those breasts, disciples wouldn't know where to look!' A pause and then in a hectoring tone, 'Mary Magdalene was, is, a completely different kettle of fish. She was an acknowledged tart turned good.' His hand began to stray to his groin and he grabbed himself violently and squeezed until tears prickled in his eyes.

'Down boy, down.' He let go of himself. 'Our father who art in heaven, hallowed be thy name, thy kingdom come, thy will be done, on earth as it is in heaven… no, I know it doesn't do any good, but it does take my mind off it.' He didn't sound convincing and his next action proved the point. Placing both hands on the seat, he began to thrust his pelvis up and down, back and forth, and began to sing quite beautifully, 'I'm too sexy for Barbara, too sexy for her height, too sexy for her breasts.' He broke off swiftly. 'What were we talking about? Yes, yes, that's right, Descartes, conceptual philosophy. No proof, no grounding.' He thumped his hand on his knee. 'No, he is not worth discussing. Now Poppy, that's a different issue. But that reminds me, before we get onto him, have you noticed, yes you, the amount of tropical vegetation that is occurring in our green and glorious land?' Again he cocked his head to listen. 'Of course, I know it's global warming, I do read *The Guardian*, cover to cover, every single day, for my penance. What a rag, full of propaganda, worse than the government. Worse than that would-be Conservative, Blair.' He took a huge breath, 'Blair without a care, Blair without a care, vote for Paddy Pantsdown 'cos what you see is what you get!'

He was beginning to rant, his cheeks began to redden, his eyes to flicker. Again his hand strayed to his groin and he grabbed at himself viciously. The torrent of words ceased abruptly as he dealt with his self-inflicted pain. He released himself and I found him looking directly into my eyes.

'He said not to shout in public, don't shout in public,' he intoned, 'patronising is the word I'd use to describe him. Patronising, smug, self-congratulatory.'

All the while he was staring straight in to me. I felt I should reply, searched my mind for an appropriate response and then I realised he wasn't talking to me, he was talking through me, directly through me. I wasn't even there for him.

His eyes fidgeted away. 'It's alright for him, still practicing. Not for me.' He stopped, seeming to gather himself together, and readjusted his shirt collar, smoothed back his hair with huge sweeps of his hands and cleared his throat. Then he sat still, too still, before bending jerkily and swiftly to his carrier bag and gingerly pulling out a pair of medical gloves. He put them on, struggling. I think they must have been a small and he was definitely a medium. He delved again and brought out *The Guardian*. He shook it, taking meticulous care so that it did not touch one particle of his being.

His next words were delivered in a fast newspeak monotone. 'www.netaid.org. David Bowie, dead, George Michael, dead, The Corrs, all dead except the violinist, saved by the buoyancy of her breasts, Catatonia, dead due to fat, Robbie Williams, dead, Bryan Adams, dead white, but dead. 80,000 in the audience, all dead. Prince Charles, dead, Camilla Parker Bowles, dead... stupid after wasting £150,000 on her well-being for the year. Paddington passengers, dead, all dead.' This was followed by a huge sigh.

He folded the newspaper precisely and returned it to his bag. He kept his medical gloves on though and began to stroke his arm with them, cooing softly, playing the child. He moved his hands slowly and seductively to his legs and began to stroke himself knee to groin, again and again.

'Naughty, naughty, naughty Nigel,' his rich chuckle burst forth at his admonishment of himself. And then wistfully, 'Wish I had breasts, then I could just play all the while. Never bother anyone then. My own titties, jubblies, pyramids, jugs, milk bottles, wobblers, my very own big round breasts.' He lapsed into silence for a short while, until, in falsetto, he began to sing again. 'The hills are alive with the sound of music, ah, ah, ah, ah. Music, a child who learns music is statistically proven to be a faster student in every other subject.' He shook his head at his invisible companion. 'No, that's a fact,' he listened. 'Fact!' He listened again before screaming, 'It is a fact, you ignorant bastard!'

And then he began to cower, to whimper as though blows were raining upon him. 'Sorry, sorry, didn't mean to raise my voice.' He squirmed and wriggled, his body contorting in imagined agony.

I felt so helpless. I sat in rigid immobility merely observing his pain.

He stopped, sat up straight and assumed a calming doctor's voice, 'Nigel where's your tablets? Um? Where's your tablets? Take one, there's a good chap.' He put his hand into his jean pocket and came out with a packet of Anadin. He methodically popped the pills from their silver cocoon into his rubber-gloved hand. I counted six, seven, eight, nine. He then put them all in his mouth and began to chew. His face twisting with the bitter taste, he began to gag but persisted in his chewing and laborious swallowing all of them.

'Nasty,' was his only comment.

The Tube slowed as we approached Warren Street. He looked at me, leaned towards me, smiled beautifically and asked, 'Am I right in thinking the next stop is Euston?'

I think he was talking to me, not through me, 'Ah no, I think it's Warren Street.' I replied a little nervously.

'No, I don't think so. I think you'll find it will be Euston, I get off here all the time, so I should know!' and then he yelled at me, 'Shouldn't I?'

'Yes,' I murmured.

As he got off at Warren Street he turned to give me a friendly wave. Then stood on the platform. As the train moved off, he banged on the window at me, waved, smiled and shouted: 'Cheerio, lovely to have met you!' He began to jog alongside the carriage, 'Have a nice day!' And the train sped up and left him behind.

The First Worst Thing

by
Andrew

Ah, the eighties. Seems like ages ago. Or was it just yesterday?
And for some reason I decided to make the protagonist female.
She reminded me of a girlfriend I once had, all those years ago.
I wonder where she is now?

Remember how you were when you were young? Innocent?
Trusting? OK, maybe not you. But I was. And then the
adult world crowds in and you end up doing things you're
ashamed of. Sometimes I get asked, "What's the worst thing
you've ever done?" And to be honest I can't recall. But I do
remember my first worst thing.

I was sixteen and really chuffed with my first proper job
after "O" levels. The department store was in the city centre
and I loved learning about all the make-up and perfumes.
And the other girls. Wow. They were just so... glossy. I had
a long way to go to catch up. But maybe it was that innocent
difference that made me attractive.

I made some friends there too. I didn't realise how
poisonous they could be until later. But by then I had a bit
of a bite myself. My best friend was Mandy on the L'Oreal
counter. I worked over the aisle and we were always giggling
at what the customers wore, or if any tasty men came in. We
had a rating system for the men. After some experimentation
we agreed on animals. So a hot black guy might be a panther.
An East End geezer might be a stray cat. Or a dog would be,
well, a dog. At the start Mandy was much better at this than
me. Others not in on the joke would always wonder why we
were talking about wildlife and then falling about. That made
it even more fun, especially in the staff canteen.

One guy did suss us though. Taylor. He became a friend.
He fancied Mandy but he and I made a connection. Same

sense of humour, I think. One day, he took me to the basement where he watched CCTV pretty much all the time with two others, looking for shoplifters and greedy staff. It was him who showed me the blind spot in my section. They were all over the place these blind spots. Taylor said the store didn't invest enough in technology. Sometimes, just for a laugh, when I was on my counter, I'd look up at the camera and wave to him. Then I'd disappear into the blind spot and come back seconds later and poke my tongue out. My attempt at flirting I guess, even though he didn't always see me.

I'd been in the job for about two months and one day this gorgeous man came onto Cosmetics. A stallion, Mandy and I agreed. Very well groomed. He worked on the second floor. Mandy said he was a buyer and going places upstairs. About thirty. Lovely suit. Sleek hair. And I've always liked a man who knows his scents. That day it was Armani. Some men swamp themselves but on him it was just enough. And amazingly as he walked past, he caught my eye and came over. For me. Me, not Mandy for once.

"Hey, where have they been hiding you?"

I know. It sounds so naff now. I must have given some lame reply but it didn't put him off.

"I'll have to spend more time down here in future. As long as you promise never to change."

"Oh, I'm preserved in amber." It wasn't long after the first *Jurassic Park* film had come out so my head was full of how they made the dinosaurs. He gave me a slightly quizzical look, but followed it up with such a sexy smile and that was it, instant obsession. Then off he went, back to heaven. Or at the very least the second floor.

Mandy was a bit quiet after that. She was so used to being the man magnet. I hate to say it but a little thrill went through me, enjoying her discomfort. Finally, I was becoming as glossy as the others!

Alex came to see me quite often after that. Always looking super smart and smelling yummy. Always a nice word for me. He filled my thoughts and, yes, my fantasies. The poor boy who'd been trying to make faltering conversation on the station platform every morning now got my cold shoulder. He was like a scraggy meerkat next to my beautiful stallion.

One day at work, Mandy came over all conspiratorial.

"That Alex you like so much – I've just heard he was a real shit to Tracy in Chinaware. Nearly raped her he did. She's so upset she's given in her notice."

Well, Mandy's gossip wasn't welcomed by me at all. Oh no. And I knew Tracy, just a little.

"Maybe she gave him the wrong idea. Serves her right for sticking those boobs she's so proud of into every man's face."

Mandy, who was not adverse to a bit of boob sticking herself, didn't take it kindly.

"What, you'd believe that git over Tracy?"

"Yes I would. And Tracy needs to get a decent bra. She's already got a bad case of the droop."

That's what I'd been thinking about Mandy to be quite honest. Mandy gave me a look and walked off. That was the end of our animal magic. I didn't care. Surely Alex would ask me out soon.

And he did. After one of his regular fly-bys. He made a bit of small talk as always and turned to go. Then: "Oh me and some of the guys are going to The Phoenix tonight. Come along if you're free."

The rest of the day I was so excited. And then I started to panic. Did I look OK? Money was always tight but I had to treat myself to a new lipstick. Had to look good. Alex had asked me to meet him inside. I fought my way through the crowd. The place was packed with retail bunnies. Alex was with some people from marketing. He had a seat but I didn't mind standing. I didn't understand what they were talking about most of the time, but it all sounded like it was from another world. God knows how much I drank. For some reason, Alex wanted me to drink cider and every time my glass was half empty another bottle would appear. I was quite tipsy when Alex asked me if I was hungry and did I fancy Italian? Alex said his goodbyes to the other guys. What all the winking was about I had no idea.

We got to this Italian place a few steps away. My eating out experience at the time peaked at McDonald's or Pizza Hut, so the big menus and bottles with straw round them made me feel like I was on holiday. Alex seemed to know all the waiters and in between talking to them he would give me sexy looks. Him and the staff were all voting about something and I think the result was a six. Then they started talking about sports and discussing if it was a goer. They all seemed to agree it was. I don't remember eating, but I do remember Alex was keen on topping up my wine glass. I was floating and even when he said he believed in going Dutch, it didn't burst my bubble. I said I didn't know what Dutch was but it sounded a bit rude. He got all the waiters over to share that one and how they all laughed. I did too. More laughter when the bill came, and I realised I had to give him twenty pounds towards his share, as payroll had mucked up his money again that month. Poor Alex.

He suggested we go back to his car. Oh my God, I didn't realise he was going to drive me home. I was quite relieved as it was a long haul on the Tube at night and I never felt safe with all those drunks about. And my mum would be worried. Ever since her stroke she'd got anxious about me, plus I always had to help her into bed.

When Alex asked me to get in the backseat I thought he was such a gentleman – it would be like having my own private driver. So, when he got in next to me, I was a bit surprised. Then I realised, of course, he wanted a kiss and a cuddle. Well, I wasn't a prude and not quite born yesterday, so it seemed fair enough. He was smelling sweet, although there was another stale smell from somewhere inside the car that I didn't like, and the leather was cold and there was a pizza box and some tissues on the floor.

Well, I like a bit of a fumble like any glossy shop girl but time and place and pace, you know? I went to say something like, can you turn the heating on? Then, suddenly, his cold hand was pushing up my thigh and pulling at my knickers. I just managed to push it away and then he was pawing at my blouse, trying to yank it open. It was too much and I pulled myself away, but his hand was caught and buttons went flying.

The sight of a bit of breast seemed to drive him wild and he went for me again. But I've got two brothers, so I know what to do when they go over the top. That spot just below the nose really hurts if you get it right. He sat back holding his face and swearing. Something about a prick teaser and bitch, but by then my little brain had suddenly aged five years.

The bastard had put the child locks on the back door but I screamed at him to let me out. He looked a bit sheepish, did something and the door opened.

Then I caught myself. "Alex you've ruined my blouse – I can't go home like this." And it was true. There was just one button intact at the bottom. I had a little fashion jacket on, but that wouldn't cover the evidence of our sordid thirty seconds. Nor would it do me any favours on a crowded late night Tube full of leery men. And if my mum saw me like this, she'd never let me out the house again.

"What's the problem with you girls? Lead me on all night then punch me in the face? Plenty of others who'd be happy to be in your place."

It was then I started to cry.

"I can't go home like this," I sobbed. "Look at my blouse."

"Oh for God's sake, take my scarf then! But I want it back – it's 100% cashmere, cost me eighty quid."

I took the scarf and covered myself up as best I could. I didn't want to be in the car with him any more but I couldn't bear walking the ten minutes to the station through the crowds.

"Can you just take me to the Tube?"

"Well I would, but I'm a bit low on the old petrol."

I got home OK, although it was the last train. My tears had been replaced by a dirty used feeling that I'd not had before. But by morning I felt a bit guilty. Maybe I had been leading him on a bit. Maybe I had drunk a bit too much. I shouldn't really have hit him so hard. And he was such a sexy guy. If he'd just warmed me up for ten minutes or so it could have all turned out differently.

In that frame of mind, I arrived at my counter. But before I could even start sorting product, Mandy was in my face. Another girl was with her. I recognised her as someone who had only started last week. I had just a moment to wonder what on earth she was wearing on her face – those colours were a big mistake – when Mandy started.

"Nice time with Alex last night?" she sneered.

"Lovely, thank you."

"Hmm, I don't think he feels the same way. He told Lily here to tell you that you shouldn't play big girls' games and he wants his scarf back."

My softer mood evaporated and was replaced by something harder which festered and bubbled nastily until lunchtime. I didn't know what I was going to do. I did know I'd want an audience.

I'd had my break when he turned up. He was looking great as usual, and today it was Guerlain Samsara. He was carrying one of our store bags. Plonking it down on the counter he gave me a look. Before I could say anything, Mandy called over to him.

"Present for me?"

My heart leapt. He'd got me a little gift to say sorry. Forgiveness welled in my silly shop girl heart.

"Ha, you wish! Just treated myself to a new Mount Blanc pen."

"Ooh, lets see," squealed Mandy, and both her and little miss crowded round as Alex showed off his newest status symbol.

"Look, it writes beautifully," I heard Alex say. And then I swear I saw him write his phone number with it and pass it over to Mandy with a wink.

Any thoughts of forgiveness died, leaving a little cancer behind in what remained of my innocent heart. Shame his car didn't run on ink. Shame my twenty pounds had gone towards his stupid pen. My gaze turned to the store bag he'd left on the counter. I suddenly realised we were right by the blind spot. I didn't think it through. I moved the bag towards the end of the counter, faded into the blind spot and pulled three cartons of Crème de la Mer moisturizer from the shelf. I threw them into the store bag, and then shoved Alex's precious eighty pound cashmere scarf on top.

At last, Mandy finished her fawning over the pen and Alex came over.

"Got my scarf?" No sorry, no small talk, no nothing. Just like we'd gone back in time before the night before. Any hesitation about what I was doing vanished.

"In the bag." He glanced inside and gave me a little smile.

"Bad girl." He didn't yet realise quite how bad. Then he was off.

The alarms kicked in as soon as he left the floor. At least the company had invested in that much technology. Those cartons were worth sixty pounds each, so like all high-end products, had alarm tags.

He looked confused for a moment but kept going. He hadn't got more than ten paces when Security was on him. The store bag was put on a nearby counter and emptied. And by that time everyone was looking. Me, Mandy, the new bad colours girl, and all the staff who had an eye-line. Then Taylor turned up, and someone in plain clothes who I never even realised worked for us. And off they went, Alex looking red as a beetroot and protesting. I suspect even the Samsara didn't keep him smelling sweet when they took him to the security room and he realised his job and career were quickly slipping away.

Taylor came to see me later. Something about the CCTV not looking that conclusive. But he could fix it if I did him a favour. Without realising what debt I was getting into, I agreed. I felt shaky but determined to get my revenge.

I think my second husband summed it up when he said I didn't trust men. But you can't blame me. Can you?

Ten Second Rule

by
Andrew

Pretty much all the men I know under the age of fifty have a rule a bit similar to this. It only changes when you get older, uglier and more desperate.

If you don't fancy her in the first ten seconds then forget it.

The rule had served David well during his 19 months of assorted internet, speed and dinner dating. If it was a first meet like this one, you knew in ten seconds. That was the rule. His mate Mike insisted it was three seconds but David was nothing if not big-hearted and added the extra seven just in case. Then a quick coffee on him – never booze – and finally The Speech.

"Listen, (insert name – the flirting course had said to always use the name) you're really nice and it was lovely to meet you. Not sure if there's a chemistry. More about me than you. But I'm sure you'll find the right one soon. Good luck with the job/decorating/shopping for your sister's birthday. Got to shoot." Little peck and away.

He was always good at listening and picking up on something he could throw in to make the rejection a bit less hurtful. For her and for him. God knows he didn't want to be seen as anything other than nice. He wasn't a bastard like some of the men the women on the dates sometimes told him about.

Of course, some dates happily passed the 10 second rule. And turned into second dates, and third, and meals and sex. But, mysteriously, rarely much further. It was just that the right one had never appeared. And after all, the choice was great. This was a big city with lots of women out there in industrial quantities. And he didn't look too bad. He was tall enough to overcome most women's horror of a small man, never wore comedy ties, didn't collect railway timetables, had a lopsided easy smile, decent job, two legs and more than half a brain.

So here he was with – God, was it Jackie or Jacqueline? Well, anyway, whoever it was, she hadn't passed the ten seconds, and there they were in a coffee chain, him with a tea, her with a ridiculous looking hot chocolate loaded with cream. Well, at least she was getting through it quickly and soon he could move to The Speech.

"You don't fancy me, do you?" This wasn't supposed to happen.

"No, it's not that. You're nice looking. But not sure the chemistry is quite right." Good improvising there he thought, using extracts from The Speech in context.

"What part of the chemistry, exactly? Is it the carbon? Or the potassium and zinc mix not quite right? Electrolytes wonky? Come on, you can tell me." Uh oh. Bit of an eccentric one here. Still, at least it had woken him up.

"Electrolytes are fine but maybe they need a bit more of a charge." That didn't come out quite right. He hoped it wasn't going to lead to a row with a near stranger in a public place.

"Well, we can charge them up a bit so you like them more." She lifted her leg and draped it over his, banging the chair of the next table and bringing a glance from the busy Mr Laptop.

What to do now? Remove it or just look at it like a fool? He looked at it. It was actually quite nice and there was the thigh not previously seen under the knee length skirt. She wiggled it about.

"We can go nuclear if you like. Let me just take off my glasses and you can observe the results."

"Isn't nuclear dangerous? What about radiation?" Hah! He could play this game too!

"Sod the risks I say. Maybe I'll grow another breast. That'll make this date more interesting." She flung her glasses onto the table then dipped her fingers into the remnants of the creamy hot chocolate and rubbed them around her lips. "They've exposed innocent dogs to radiation and apart from a little rabies, they were fine." She blew and a little cream bubble appeared at one corner of her mouth.

He couldn't help laughing and the next moment they were both giggling. Mr Laptop got up and walked away. That made them giggle a bit more.

"It's the men who are supposed to be funny, you know." Well, that was true, wasn't it?

"Oh! Is there a rule?" She looked at him with comic indignation. He'd not really noticed her eyes before. Very dark. And big. "Are you a rule man? As a rule? Do you always smell your socks before you put them on? Do you have a rule about tucking your shirts in before you do up your belt? Do you have a rule about taking first dates to a naff coffee shop before you dump them?" Ouch. How could he tell her he was a nice guy really?

"I wasn't going to dump you!"

"No? But what about the signs? I know about these male signs. I've read the books. That little look of disappointment in the first glance. Men are so visual! Then the looking around. I saw you looking at that black girl when you were in the queue. When you should have been looking at me." It was true.

"You're the proper detective." Maybe a bit defensive – but not too bad.

"I am. But I don't want the cold cases. And you said the chemistry wasn't right. You can't argue with the forensic evidence." With that she removed her warm leg from his, recovered her glasses and stood.

"Hey, don't go! I thought we were having fun." And he had been having fun. For once.

"Some fun, maybe. But I've got a rule for dates. Don't want to waste your time or mine if we can't charge the electrolytes."

She gave him a quick peck and walked off.

"Wait, Jackie!" But she didn't.

"It's Jacqueline." And she was out the door and away.

He had a miserable evening after that. She hadn't responded to his funny text about atoms. Should he leave a voicemail? Damn his silly rules.

Friday Twilight

by
Janet

The pressure we put on ourselves, at work and at play, the daily stress of living in a buzzing city. To counter this I began to imagine an earthbound Nirvana. But the story ending took me by surprise even as I was writing it!

Muggy evening. Friday twilight, women's wearied bodies, pollutant full, jerk and chug and slowly move from city core to city sides. Tired business folk, clad in once pressed business suits, now limp and crumpled, concertinaed into wrinkles that are reflected in the lines amassing around their eyes, lines too early for their years. Paperwork out in diligent duty at 7-Eleven at the week's end is held immobile, on top of briefcases, on top of tired knees.

And the knees! Eyelids flicker and sigh into closure and paperwork slips to the ground – eyes snap wide, papers are regained in startled fashion and shoved into cases that are shoved onto floors – and eyelids fall again, against their owners will, to shut the work away. And the heads loll and the necks sag and the knees begin to splay, splayed and held by confines of skirt seams – still wide enough to glimpse the stocking tops.

Night men, male murkers, know the time to sit and see and sit across and wait on twilight Friday tired-time. They sit across and lower in their seats to view a thigh 'bove stocking top.

Jolt, jerk, train doors shriek apart. Hurried awake, women of weariness rush from seat to platform, grabbing at pens and glasses and papers and jackets and thoughts and tumble onto platforms. Screech, clash and the train creaks into action and disappears as women smooth their dresses, straighten shoulders, hitch down hems, push tiredness away.

Clippity-clop to the one working escalator, clippity-clop and stop, too exhausted to partake of free exercise to walk the moving stairwell. Straggling through barriers, they shuffle the solid stairs, up and into the fresh air of eventime.

Let's you and I follow but one. Umm. Maggie.

Ah see, the Fishmongers van still parked. She's buying dead fish and sea vegetables before trekking on painful heels towards a relaxing weekend, slowing, as relaxing seeps her mind-ways. That's right, the wine bar tonight to see Tonia and Mary and Jane. What time? Was it eight-thirty? Exhaustion digests memory. Time now? Seven forty-five, in real time seven-forty, those added five minutes on the clock face prevent tardiness – the scourge of the unprofessional business being. Just time to shower and scrub up into weekend wear. Time to let her hair down, slip into slinky, add iridescent make-up for the illusion of vigour.

Maggie unlocks once, twice, thrice the doorway to her home. A nasty neighbourly note crouches at the entrance poised to snap at her toes. Unfolded, scrawled in spider-hand: 'Rubbish is removed every Monday as you well know, solicitors will be contacted if you do not abide by this rule.

The Residents of Sunnyview Court.

P.S. Please pick up your existing rubbish strewn by the fox!'

The phone begins to jangle. Maggie screws and drops the note and drops her supper upon the hallway floor, as she lunges, leaping over the weeks' accumulated debris to stop its clamour.

'You bitch, you bitch, you bitch!' Brrrr.

Ah, the ex before the ex before the ex. Maggie sighs, jaded by a phrase that is beginning to sound of truth.

Kicks off shoes, strips off suit, strips, strips down to the bone that never sees sunlight now; nor exercise, muscles withering in wobble at only thirty-two. She pads to the ansaphone, four messages. Should she? Is there a choice?

Click:

Mother: Sister's upset, still no sign of a card, remember it's an achievement to produce a child.

Boss: Maggie, are you there? Damn!

Sandra: (Tearful) Can't make Sunday, too much work again.

Boss: Maggie, where the hell are you? Call as soon as you get home, I'm here till eleven.

Oh the courage to ignore, but no, fingers dial automatically. 'Bob? – Maggie… yes… yes… yes… yes… yes.'

And half an hour has passed, of chit of chat of lists of Monday things to do that could perhaps be started on the morrow? Keep the client, make the client extra happy. And now her watch says eight-twenty. Maggie steams into a shower of cold needles that wash away tears of absolute fatigue. She struggles and struggles into slinky, over still damp skin. Have to take care now. Just time to brush the hair violently, upside down, pink in the face, hair full of static, ah yes, the illusion of vitality has been achieved, for the moment. Grabs keys, grabs purse, grabs bag, grabs make-up, grabs smile and slams out.

And the dead fish begins its rot in the hallway, slowly forming pusses of putrification.

First traffic lights, mascara, second traffic lights, lipstick, a routine tried and tested too many times to count. Squeeze into parking space, breeze into wine bar, shriek, release, yeh, yeh, yeh, the weekend starts here!

And here! And here! And here! And here and wine and more wine and wild, wilder women – hungry, hungry, wild straight shots to the bloodstream of vodkas and snakebites and oh and oh and any and everything. Conversations mostly of shout and blur. The faces of Tonia and Mary and Jane, swim and recede and bloat and contract, giggles and tears, all girls together, they tip over into the drunken hunt for a fella.

Maggie feels: man? No breasts, must be, must be, kiss and slobber, sees disconnected eyelashes one upon one, lips loose, nose pores expanding with heating desire and silvered saliva passes one to the other, all images lead to her funnel, her tunnel of escape. Escape in the front of, in the front of everyone, she thinks, she screams the thought aloud in the drunken parody of her furried mind. She screams without sound, I'm not alone, am I? Am I? I'm a good time, fun-time girl, full of vivacity, joviality. Watch me my girlfriends, see, see, envy my popularity. Please, please…

And then time blots and blacks away and it is tomorrow, that early time synonymous with the chorus of dawn birds, and the pounding, and the pounding of Maggie's head. The familiar Saturday tattoo. In gentleness she tests her neck, her constant thump of tension, a juddering roll to the right, a juddering roll to the left – unknown hair sprouts from the duvet. The Saturday sinking, who came home last night, what lecherous man enticed her to her bed? Maggie remembers nothing – nothing, but glasses up-tipping, clinking and chinking against teeth.

Dry mouth, sodden bladder urges attention. Maggie slides with practiced quietude, pads in fragile fashion to the door, opens it silently. Retches involuntarily at the stench, the overriding stench of fish. Makes it to the bathroom and vomits, and vomits, and vomits, gallons of red soured wine, laced with froth of vodka. Gazes in the mirror at bloodstained eyes, examines the concentric semi-circles of dark unhappiness underlying them. Sighs, what else is there to do?

Flushes once then empties bladder, tries to de-fur tongue. Wraps soggy towel to cover tired flesh. Gingerly approaches hallway, picks up at arm's length fish that's turning into fluid in plastic bag and tries to ram, ram, ram it into kitchen bin, already overflowing with packages of micro-ed yesterdays. Attempts a glass of water with two Anadin extra; three sips only before her stomach lurches treacherously.

Pads back to bed to sleep and sleep and sleep into oblivion. She slides in, a hand shoots out to encircle her waist. Oh God, oh God, they always want it in the morning – best do it, get it over, get it done with no chit, no chat, then sleep. The hand surprises into soft caress, muffled appreciation emits from the duvet, any moment now Maggie knows the heave and the shove will commence, lubrication missing, soreness unremitting. Stiff in stillness Maggie awaits her onslaught. But the hand surprises by demanding nothing and Maggie and the man slick into slumber until the phone by the bed jangles at one twenty-seven pm. But the breast is brushed, so gently, so gently. The body pulls itself alongside murmuring, murmuring: 'Lovely, lovely.' Maggie holds interminable breath – it is the voice belonging to a woman!

How drunk had she been? How craving for affection? How desperate for human touch, the brush of lips, the hug and the hug and the need and the need and the endless need to be, to be loved, question mark? Isn't she? Aren't I? Maggie's question hangs in her mind. How sad I am she berates, how pathetic and what's her name? The foreign fingers are still exploring, now the valley between her breasts. Maggie knows not how to stop them nor does she want… dot, dot, dot… She locks off her mind and floats on the touches of featherlight. They are as whispers of a touch, not of demand and supply as of usual encounters of the sexual kind, but gossamer, subsuming. Maggie dare not look upon the perpetrator, knowing the spell would splinter.

A flutter kiss touch-tingles upon Maggie's neck to Maggie's core, and Maggie's body begins to ease into openness. No battle, no bristle, no stubble, pleasure pieces built on pieces of pure pleasure. The softness of a melting breast, flattening, flowing around her ribs, fingers all the time tender touch with their tips, stray over belly, explore thigh top that male murkers have spied and died to thrust against and in.

But this Siren parts Maggie's legs in smooth gentleness, circles and rubs, finds the hub, lips gently gliding over breasts, and after forever time insinuates sex against sex. Maggie feels and frees and floats and releases and releases and cries out before her weeping begins, before she holds the unknown woman to her hard and hard with caring.

More sleep, blissful slumber.

Awakens to a shoulder touch, a smile, a cup of tea proffered, sound of bath running.

Then softly: 'I'm Zoe, thanks for inviting me back.' The vision smiles, Maggie's heart explodes with love.

Still Got It Going On

by
Andrew

At some stage, men have to give themselves a good talking to and decide to grow up. But some never get round to it. I see them in Wetherspoons at 11.30 on a Tuesday morning with a pint. As I'm passing by, of course.

Sixty, I've still got it going on,
Even after my girlfriend's gone,
She told me I was sad
But no, I'm a boy who still is bad.

Gonna go out and hit the scene,
No way I'm a has-been,
She'll see - won't take me long,
Coz I still got it going on.

Gonna find me some hot laydeez,
Who won't give me no maybeez,
Sidle up in the club and say hey,
No pause, they'll just say, 'OK.'

I'll take em back to, well, I dunno,
My ex she kicked me out you know,
But my mum's got a spare room,
And she's at the care centre all Tuesday
        afternoon.

Oh, it will be a steamy session,
But first I have to impress them
With tales of how bad was my ex,
Get that out the way before we have sex.

Then we'll get down to some good fine
        loving,
I'll take my back pain relief belt off and do
        all the pushing and shoving,
I'll get her there real fast and hear her moan,
Coz I still got it going on.

Then, perhaps a quick fag,
With the window open as mum's a bit of
        a nag,
And maybe this new girl will have a place,
That I can just go to, whenever I need
        some space.

My ex said I was a dirty selfish old git,
Just coz I touched that young neighbour up
        a bit,
Talk about blowing things up out of
        proportion,
Is what I told them down at the police
        station.

And when the ex sees how well I'm moving
Just you wait, she'll come running back for
        some of my good loving,
But I might play hard to get,
Make her work for it – you bet!

But, before she does I'll enjoy my single
        ways,
Get down the Wetherspoons early to plan
        my days,
Oh, it's gonna be so much fun,
Coz I still got it going on.

Aghast

by
Janet

Love only happens to the beautiful people, or so the glossy magazines lead us to believe. I wanted love to blossom with real people.

'Annie.'

'A, n, double n?'

'Yes.'

'Nie,' he looked up expectantly, reminiscent of a tortoise in posture, his baggy cords topped by a navy knitted waistcoat of a bygone era, although Annie supposed him to still be in his early 40s.

'I'll spell it, G H A S T.'

'G H,' he muttered as he laboriously filled in the requisite card, 'A S T…A. Ghast.'

Annie hoped against hope that the inevitable wouldn't happen.

'My, that's an unusual name.'

'Yes,' said Annie briskly, trying to head him off, but for a tortoise he was fast and his repartee took her by surprise, coming from a mildly intellectual stance.

'Why, I stand in amazed terror before a woman who goes by such a name.'

'You're not the first and I'm sure not the last to feel a need to make comment upon it,' she said sharply, not wishing to prolong a conversation of such regular tedium. Although, at the same time, she recognised a kindred spirit, a lover and player of words. She turned from the counter and just as swiftly turned back. 'You never told me,' she said, 'where to find the section for poison ivy.'

Annie saw a flicker of a smile cross the librarian's face which she found intensely irritating. He sidled out from behind his protective block and began to lead her towards her request. She noticed with no sign of pity that he walked with a stoop, obviously some congenital condition she decided, lending him the air of a Dickens character.

Arriving at the Gardening section put an abrupt halt to her train of thought.

'I doubt there will be a book dedicated to Poison Ivy...'

Poison-poisson, poison-poise, poison-pose, Annie's mind whirled. How wonderful that such a word, which conjured pain and destruction, could so simply become a fish, a means of balance or adjoined to the arts.

Meanwhile, the tortoise had stopped speaking, realising that Annie was having a conversation with herself. Having been his own constant companion all his life, he recognised the signs. Instead, he observed the frayed cuffs of A. Ghast's coat and her two thin stick legs peeping from its hem, large feet encompassed in rich ox-blood leather shoes. She spent money on her feet, but not on her eyes, shielded behind NHS standard round frames, incongruous on her long narrow face.

'Were you saying something?'

'Yes, you might want to look in the more esoteric sections; it may have been used in various spells.'

Esoteric, mulled Annie, esoteric-easy, esoteric-so, esoteric-Teric, was there a man's name Teric, or was it Tariq?

The tortoise smiled to himself and limped away towards the Music section. This woman intrigued him, he'd like to get to know her over time. He picked out *The Anthology of the Rolling Stones* and flicked to the index. Yes there, *Poison Ivy*, recorded '67. He limped back towards Gardening. And perhaps she would like to get to know him; the substance, not the shell of him.

Bushfire

by
Janet

I was on a three-month holiday in Adelaide, Australia. I was amazed by the frequency and severity of the fires there and the relentless news bulletins giving constant updates.

Thirty-eight degrees. Stultifying. My white dress clings wetly to my body as I wait for the bus, my back to the hills. I don't move, not even my eyes. I just stand, hatless in the heat.

The bus wheezes into view and squelches to a stop. No air-conditioning I realise as I climb the steep steps. The driver is glaring at me as I fumble nervously with my purse, the fetid stench of sweat curling around me from his dripping shirt. I feel a glimmer of recognition, that surly mouth hiding in the tangle of his beard knocks my memory.

It's four o'clock. The bus is crammed with squirming, squealing school children. I collapse into the only available seat, near the front – on the left. My feet are resting on the vibrating wheel hub.

There is an overweight blonde sitting behind the driver. I can see an ugly repair to the seam on the underarm of her tight pink dress, tattily done in strong black thread. She looks as uncomfortable on the outside of her body as I feel on the inside of mine.

I drift away. I see the cool turquoise of the ocean on my left. I see the water flat and rippleless, the blue sky stretching on endlessly. But these I know are merely conjuring tricks, sleight of hand, to give the impression of tranquillity and order. I play a game with myself; if I only look to the left and believe in the magic, everything will turn out right for me.

The driver suddenly clicks on the news, blasting my eardrums with the volume.

In panic, I realise I don't want to hear it. I want him to switch if off. I pray; please God, make him switch it off.

The newsreader's voice is sharp and clinical. I hold my breath. I already sense the news he is about to relay. A fire at Kuitpo Forest.

The voice clips on dispassionately. The fire has now spread to six sites, forty fire-trucks are in attendance. The wind is increasing. One house has been razed to the ground. There is one unidentified, known fatality.

The driver angrily tells the bursting pink lady his house is in the middle of the fires. I place him now, we live in the same area. He carries on. I strain forward to hear the conversation. He feels sorry for the poor victim, but he's glad it's not one of his family. The fires started at half past one. The Cherry Gardens blaze had to be left unattended, not enough fire trucks. At two, he called his wife to take the kids, leave their house and meet him in the city.

The driver is frantic. I am gleeful. Hugging knowledge to myself like a miser.

I know who the fatality is.

And knowing, I have the courage to turn my head to the right. My eyes take in the dry barrenness of the summer landscape, where plumes of purple smoke are pushing and punching endlessly into the sky. Swollen, heavy, painful, just like the bruises hidden beneath my dress.

There are no red flames, only the suffocating smoky results scratching across the sky. I watch the polluting clouds, belching upwards, crowding to block out the sun, the light of life, to crush out the day, to bring an early brutish twilight, cobalt blue.

A giggle sweeps through me. I trap it in my throat. Here I am, caught in a web of time, in my bus journey from Aldinga. Trapped between cool sea and furious fire. Suspended in time. Responsible for nothing. As yet unfound.

Who would have thought? Simple things learnt so innocently at school, a cunningly placed magnifying glass, positioned to ignite the dry grass in the sizzling midday sun.

The unseen flames have freed me from that rancid body, that twisted mind, dreaming along alcoholic tunnels of ugliness. That drunken sot, lying stinking in his continual stupor of drink, his violence stemmed only in heaving, snoring sleep, has been cooked into death.

My bullying husband charred and preserved in an agony of fear and flame. Just another unfortunate bushfire fatality.

I want to laugh out loud.

But no. I must wait. I must be controlled. I must also remember to murmur a word of condolence to the driver when I leave the bus.

Trafalgar Square Moment

by
Andrew

I saw a video of tribal mob election violence in Kenya and some of the images are still burned on the back of my eye. And then I was out for a walk in Greenwich Park and someone yelled, "Finborough! Come here!" And the story was born.

"Finborough! Tuscany!" The mother's high voice cut through the late afternoon. "Play indoors now – we can't have you getting chills." Reluctantly the twins left the rambling back garden and returned to the house, on the promise that Kiki would fix them her special "African snack".

As she heard this, Kiki stiffened. But she was nothing if not robust. Making toasted cheese sandwiches with Nutella (an accidental hit with the kids) was better than being raped and watching your brother being hacked to death by a machete.

Kiki wasn't her real name. She was a Kikuyu from Kenya and something in her naïve description of tribal history had got lost in translation during the domestic agency interview. But it was easy for the twins to pronounce and now that her English was better, she realised there was no point in asserting her true identity. Who would care? This was Greenwich, a wealthy London suburb where African domestics abounded with few questions asked.

Snacks made, she went back to the utility room but was interrupted again. "Kiki sweetie, I know you've got your hands full but could you take the car in for a service tomorrow? Martin's got another bloody meeting and I simply must go to the gym. You can manage it all right, can't you?"

Kiki nodded. She had no license but it was always better to say yes to these distant, nearly nice people.

A wonderful feeling of power came over Kiki as she steered the huge black 4x4 onto the A2. Her family had been farmers and her father had let her drive the pick up before that too was burnt by the tribal mob, with him still inside. And auto was easy.

The satnav directed her into a side street. She caught her breath, for there, shambling across the road with a yellow bucket, mop and matching plastic gloves was the mob leader from her village, whose mocking face, rotten breath and smoky aroma she would never forget. After the tribal madness, both victims and aggressors sought asylum in the West. She briefly remembered Martin had said if you sat in Trafalgar Square long enough you would see everybody you'd ever met. She'd actually gone once on one of her lonely free Sundays and only seen strangers, but supposed that now her Trafalgar moment had finally come.

Kickdown in auto was sublime. By the time her revenge connected, her speed was seventy. She thought she'd dragged him a little way after too. Good.

A quick car wash tidied things up. The garage said it needed a new front bumper and she said fine. Martin never looked at the bills.

That night she slept without the dreams. Awaking, she resolved that now, at last, she could go home.

The L Word

by
Andrew

My therapist, if I had one, would say this story was my way of processing a relationship. The road rage incident nearly happened but didn't. So I took it to an alternate universe where it did.

I'm good at getting women. Not boasting, it's a fact. The formula's simple. Listen, laugh and love. I ease off on these three Ls once I've got them hooked in. That's because of the fourth. Lazy. It's a character weakness, I know. Sooner or later that activates the fifth, which of course is Leaving. That's never bothered me until recently. I know I can always get a replacement, whenever I want. But maybe because I'm now in my fifties a new L has started to come in. Loneliness. That was never part of the plan. But you can't teach an old dog new tricks. That's why there I was, being Lazy with Bev, one Saturday afternoon.

"I want to talk."

Uh oh, here we go, I thought. Bad news on the way. I wasn't quite ready to leave this one just yet. And I like to have control over the timing.

"Sure," I replied, "but can we wait until the cricket's finished?"

"No, I'd really like to talk now, please."

It was the 'now' that made me look up from the TV. It'll be the 'where are we going' talk, I thought.

"Tony, where are we going? It'll be a year in June."

I turned the cricket down a bit. "Bev, do we have to be going somewhere? Although I'm always happy to be going down the pub."

Bev was at the stage now where she ignored all my little funnies.

"Don't you love me?"

I'd made a bit of a mistake with this one and used the Love word just once quite early on, shortly after her mum had died and she was in a bit of a state. Now she'd brought it up, it lay steaming on the carpet between us.

"Well…" I took a deep breath.

"No, it's all right Tony. I'm not going to force you to say anything you don't want to." I looked at her and could see first stage tears start to download. OK, I know. I'm a bastard. But I've had many women cry on me over the years, so I'm an expert at spotting the early warning signs. One day, I'll post my knowledge on Wikipedia for the enrichment of mankind.

She turned away, controlling it. "I mean you don't have to love me like Romeo and Juliet. Let's be pragmatic. But neither of us is getting any younger. And I don't want to spend another two years with you and then you turn around and dump me. What a waste of time that would be for both of us."

She was right, of course. Any man with integrity and backbone would have engaged with the situation and taken the opportunity to Leave at that moment. I wasn't that man. But the truth was I liked this one, and although I was a bit bored, it still had some mileage. Plus, we had a long weekend booked in a few days, all paid for and sorted. We'd never get the money back if we cancelled now.

Before I could say anything inappropriate, she left for the bedroom, leaving me to the match. England scored a six but she'd spoiled it for me and I couldn't work up any enthusiasm. I was staying at her place for the day, so it seemed right to follow her. But I found the bedroom door almost closed. I peered through the narrow gap and could see her lying on the bed, facing the wall.

"Babes, don't get upset. Let's go have a nice little drink and a bite to eat. My treat." I said to her back.

"No, you go. I'm fine." She half turned. "Tony, don't stress yourself. It is what it is. I know that. Go and have a drink and come back, or whatever you want to do. K?"

"K." I let myself out quietly. When I got back later, it seemed like it was all forgotten and we had a cuddle on the sofa. I relaxed a little. Our long weekend was probably going to be all right.

The day of the trip came round soon enough, and there we were, driving in my little sports car, roof off, music playing, heading towards Norfolk, both cheerful. We hadn't gone more than two miles from my South London place when I got to the right turn I'd taken a million times before. Indicating, I got in lane. The lights were green, should be able to make it through before they turned, I thought, in that unconscious way we all have when we're driving in familiar territory. I put on a little burst of speed just to make sure. The second I accelerated the lights went to amber. Something in the configuration of the cars waiting to go on the other side unnerved me. It looked like the white van man was going to pull away like a loony and I didn't want to be crossing his path. Shit. I braked hard and we came to a sudden stop just as the lights turned to red.

"Sorry babes," I said, putting a hand in front of her, even though she was wearing her belt.

A hard thud and we were both pushed back in our seats and the car skidded a foot forward.

Shit again. My heart beating fast, I looked in the mirror. An old Ford Mondeo was right up hard against my boot.

"You OK, hon?"

She nodded, looking unfazed.

"Let me sort this – just a little knock."

I got out of the car and before I'd gone a step he was in my face.

"Fucking wanker!" He pushed a fat finger hard in my chest, rocking me back. His over-red face was right in mine and I could smell bad food on his breath.

"Easy mate." I stepped back a little.

"I'm not your fucking mate! And you can't fucking drive. Tosser!" The finger was back, poking. I felt scared and angry at the same time.

"You must have been right up my arse. You shouldn't drive so close."

Wrong thing to say. He was already boiling, and this turned him up to gas mark nine.

"I'm gonna kill you!" His meaty fist connected with the side of my head. I had a mad moment to see that this bloke was about my age, but had graduated with honors from the school of hard knocks. The blow made me dizzy and I fell back against my car.

Now, I'm a lover not a fighter. I've usually got a quick comeback when dealing with the ladies but I didn't think this man would appreciate my best lines. I opened my mouth. The only word to come out was sorry. He didn't seem to hear. Wanting his pound of flesh, as if to make up for everything bad in his sad overweight life, he hit me again right in the eye. I went down, landing awkwardly on the tarmac. My expensive cream linen shirt failed to absorb the impact and I felt it rip.

This was outrageous but I was in no position to write to the newspapers about it. I was going to get a good kicking. I cowered against the side of my car, bringing my arm up to protect my face as a badly aimed kick numbed my elbow. He was screaming now, out of control, eyes bulging and a thin line of spittle threatening to disconnect from his mouth. Another kick, then a new voice. I'd forgotten Bev. She's a tiny thing but I watched amazed as she raked her sharp fingernails across his face. He stepped back, confused, and I saw four red lines on his cheek start to swell with blood. Recovering slightly, the man grabbed her wrist as she went to hit him again. With no hesitation she twisted, brought his arm up to her mouth and bit down hard. That elemental act shocked him. It certainly shocked me. He let go like she was on fire, but too slow. Her shoe smashed against his shin. I saw a look of panic cross his face and he took a couple of steps back. My girlfriend's wild shrieks followed him to his car, her high heel catching the side of his door as he reversed crazily, driving off on the wrong side of the road to the angry horns of the oncoming traffic.

By now I'd staggered to my feet and realised we'd drawn a crowd. Like a little ninja, she pulled me round the other side and pushed me into the passenger seat, then ran back to get behind the wheel. Before I could say no insurance, she was accelerating us away from my total humiliation. After about a mile we stopped outside a Tesco Express and she came back with a mini brandy and can of coke. Passing me the brandy, she took a big swig from the can, rolled it around her mouth and spat it onto the pavement.

"What did he taste like?" This was the first thing I'd said to her since the madness.

"Salty." She took another swig, gargled and spat again. Our eyes met and we both started giggling hysterically. I had a sudden thought and stopped laughing.

"You fought for me. You did. You gave it everything to save me."

"You'd do the same for me, wouldn't you?" She looked at me directly. There was a pause and I nodded, realising I meant it.

"I would if I could."

"Come on – let's go. You drive. I'm shaky, and besides, I'm not insured for your car, as you've repeatedly told me." I smiled, and we drove the rest of the way to Norfolk without fighting or blood.

I was quiet that night. We had room service to avoid the inevitable looks at my bruised face and we worked our way drunkenly through the mini bar. I woke early the next day and watched her sleeping. Suddenly moved to speak, I gently shook her awake and used the L word. She looked at me quizzically, still dozy, so I laid it on her again.

"I love you."

Not like me at all, but I really did mean it. What else could I say? After all, it's not everyday someone cares enough to fight for you tooth and claw.

Holiday: A Prequel

by
Janet

I've longed to be one of those women who always looks well turned out, hair coiffed, make-up perfect, shiny nails. But I'm not. Then I began to think about the maintenance... packing would be a nightmare.

How is it my minimalist approach to toiletries receives no complaints from the girlfriend until holiday packing time?

Shaving foam, soap, deodorant, toothpaste.

But come two weeks of Mediterranean sun and the basics no longer suffice.

The girlfriend chooses, on my behalf, shower gel, talcum powder, conditioner, shampoo, roll on anti-perspirant, all over body spray.

Anything for a quiet life. It's the hand-cream, baby lotion, sanitary towels and cotton wool that I can't find a use for.

Toothpaste could be an issue. I use Aquafresh, she Colgate. To save duplication we compromise and only take one. Colgate.

Then there's the Suntan Lotion, factors 8, 4, and 2, sun block, after sun lotion and an ointment for sunburn. Just in case.

I pack them all in my suitcase because the girlfriend can't be expected to carry these and her make-up bag as well.

No darling, I really don't mind.

To save space in my toilet bag the girlfriend employs an innovation. She treats me to a trial size shaving cream. The kind that dispenses two squirts and is then empty.

Apparently they don't do trial sizes in essentials like hairspray, hair mousse, hair wax and hair gel.

Yes Petal, I do want you to look your best.

Fortunately, I'm follically challenged, so we don't duplicate on these items.

Is there any spare room in my case?

For you sweetness, anything.

There's not enough room in her case for the ten bikinis. Experience tells me that the girlfriend will only use three at the most. It depends on what the others are wearing.

Of course, going topless means half the bikini is redundant.

No sugarplum, I'm not complaining.

Yes, I understand it's different for women.

It's the matching sarongs that I'm struggling to find room for. All the fashion, wrap-a-round sarongs. Taking ten bikinis means we need ten different matching sarongs. Makes sense.

The travel kettle in my bag?

Your wish is my command, angel.

I can never remember if electrical equipment should be packed in your hand luggage.

No matter, I use the space efficiently by putting the anti-mosquito machine inside the kettle along with the two weeks' supply of anti-mosquito tablets.

Sorry darling, you say we can't do that.

Why, light of my life?

Because you want to put the extra teabags, sweeteners and hot chocolate sachets inside the kettle.

So you suggest we leave the anti-mozzie machine behind?

That has some logic because we can then use the insect repellent spray, the insect bite cream, the anti-histamine tablets and the after bite antiseptic wipes.

You want to put the spare contraceptive pills somewhere in my case.

Of course I remember you had your handbag stolen last year with the pills inside.

True, I couldn't tell whether you had sunstroke or PMT.

No, I'm not getting flustered. I'll put them with the headache tablets, Savlon, Optrex, Diareze, emergency sterile kit, travel first aid bag, condoms, Alka Seltzer and Milk of Magnesia tablets.

You want to put the heated rollers into my hand luggage?

Anything honey-pie. And the hairdryer.

You mean the one the size of a Rolls Royce Engine?

Of course I don't mind sweetpea.

It means I only have room for two pairs of boxer shorts. But then I can make use of the bargain travel wash, and the trial size fabric conditioner – they'll smell fragrant at least – and if I rip them I can make use of the travel sewing kit.

Yes dearest, you want to put your spare make-up bag in my suitcase.

I'm confused. Is my suitcase the one with the white bras and panties or the one with coloured bras and panties?

I understand sugarpuff.

The suitcase with your shoes in, is mine? Aah, you made spare room by taking out my two pairs of jeans.

Of course I'm not moaning.

I know you need a lot of shoes to choose from.

I am trying to be helpful.

Still, the holiday's not for another three months. The girlfriend enjoys planning in advance, it gives her plenty of time to change her mind.

Carla

by
Janet

Mental health. One in four of us will experience it within our lifetimes. How does it happen? Why does it happen? Who do I know it's happened too? Will I know if it's happening to me?

Fiddling with her Elastoplast, good old dependable Carla made a decision.

Striding into her kitchen, she opened and pulled two drawers, right out of their runners, and laid them on the kitchen counter. She took out all the knives and replaced the drawers. From another she withdrew some sellotape. She then bound the blades of the knives in groups of six, over and over again. There would be no chance of further accidents. Carla then dropped them into the swing top bin and went back into the living room.

She had barely settled her rump onto the sofa when a thought struck her. It would be impossible to cut meat without knives. She strode back into the kitchen, wrenched open the freezer, and grabbing hunks of dead flesh, threw them into the gut of the swing top. Calmer, she wandered back into the living room and flicked on the TV.

For ten days her life carried on quite normally. Certain things had to be removed from the food cupboard. But she could still eat anything stored in jars or tins and, of course, fruit, nuts and raw vegetables. Carla found rolls particularly useful – although a little dry without butter.

It was early one evening, whilst munching on a carrot, that scissors snapped into Carla's mind. Two sharp edges clashing together. Carla scurried to the bathroom to find her nail scissors. Then to the desk in her lounge where lurked the paper scissors. Employing the same successful procedure as before, the blades were securely sellotaped together, over and over, before their descent into the gaping swing top.

Returning to the living room, she plonked her diminishing behind onto the sofa, emitted a comfortable sigh and resumed watching *Coronation Street*. Except it was the adverts and her straying eyes suddenly caught sight of the word at the bottom of the television set; 'SHARP'.

Her hands began to shake and she felt dizzyingly light-headed. As the strains of *Coronation Street* filled the room, Carla viciously yanked out the plug. Seizing her coat and car keys and thanking her lucky stars that she'd bought a portable, Carla proceeded to lug it downstairs. She drove erratically to her local Help the Aged, and although she knew they didn't accept electrical goods and you weren't meant to leave things in the doorway overnight, she did just that for them to stumble across in the morning.

Carla assumed that she'd be alright by the time she arrived home, but she was only able to sit a few moments before she felt compelled to find the Argos Catalogue. As she flicked through the electrical section, she couldn't bear to think she had overlooked some 'SHARP' electrical component living in her home.

She had. Her stereo! She made a repeat trip to Help the Aged, noting that the TV had already gone.

Carla slept fitfully that night, disquieted by the evening's events. The accident kept trying to push into the forefront of her mind. And she was worried about work the following day. Lunchtimes had become difficult. It was now impossible for Carla to sit at a table with knives on it. Colleagues were beginning to comment.

Carla managed to spend the lunch break alone in the office, nibbling a dry roll. She was reading the medical page of her favourite woman's magazine when, in an instant, she was drenched with sweat and consumed with terror.

The offending magazine and roll were left on the desk as she grabbed her coat and bag, flew down the stairs, through the main doors, hailed a cab and sped home.

CARLA

Once there, she rushed to the bookshelves that covered two walls of her lounge, floor to ceiling, and started throwing the books wildly onto the carpet. 'With cystitis, you may experience a sharp pain.' The phrase kept pounding in her head, like an ugly mantra. Every volume contained somewhere a sharp, cutting, slicing word to harm her, Carla knew.

Silence was pierced by the phone ringing. Carla froze and waited for the ansaphone to snap on. A voice filled the room with office concern about Carla's whereabouts. She stood stock still, barely breathing until the machine clicked off.

Then feverishly, almost maniacally, she began to take the books down to her car. She started stacking them in orderly piles, but by the eighth trip her sweaty palms and shaking limbs forced her to hurl the offending books inside. Pushing them, shoving them into every crevice and corner.

Hours later, with all the books crammed in, she squeezed herself into the Mini Metro, fighting with two stray titles that had become lodged under the pedals, she turned on the ignition and raced down to Help the Aged.

Carla drove the car onto the pavement, right alongside the shopfront, snapping off the wing mirror. She didn't notice. She struggled through the books on the passenger seat to find the door handle. The moment it swung open they started spilling onto the ground. Carla began kicking and pushing at the others, forcing them viciously out and away from her. She was grunting, but in her panic, she had no chance to stop and monitor herself. It was only when she had extracted the last of the books from under her seat, she noticed that a silent crowd had gathered, standing a discreet distance from the car.

Carla felt a flush crawl from her toes to her hairline. She slid back into the driver's seat, gunned the engine and slammed her foot on the accelerator. The unexpected noise hit the quiet street and the startled watchers backed away as Carla made a speedy escape, gouging the car paintwork against the shopfront in her haste.

Once home she sat peacefully, toying with the edges of her, by now, very grubby Elastoplast, reflecting on the turn of events since her accident.

The weekend passed uneventfully apart from a small fright on Saturday evening. Deciding on a can of vegetable soup for supper, the potential dangers of the tin opener dawned on her. Once in its sellotape caul, into the swing top bin it went. Minutes later it was buried under an avalanche of unopened tins.

Monday came round and work was tolerable. Carla excused her Friday disappearance with a migraine. This neatly stretched so that it covered her inability to answer the phone.

Apart from the voices from her clock radio, Carla was now accustomed to the silence in her flat. But the following Saturday morning, the radio news bulletin reported 'a sharp volley of shots'. It had to go!

The subsequent Sunday her filthy plaster began to peel off. Carla wound it back into place with sellotape, over and over, so that there would be no chance of even a glimpse of what lay beneath.

On the same day, all the furniture with vicious square edges began gnawing at the fringes of her mind. Dispensing of it took a little more forethought than the smaller objects. Carla unscrewed any pieces she could, until the steely sharpness of the screwdriver started searing her hand. She had to rid the flat of all the tools. She gingerly gathered them all together, tears streaking her face at the task. She left them outside the locked gates of the Municipal Dump.

On Monday morning, she made two calls. One to the office to tell them she had a tummy bug and one to Help the Aged. The warm voice at the other end expressed delight at her generosity for giving so much furniture, and arranged to send a van the following week. Instantly Carla panicked, she heard her voice spiralling higher and higher, her words tumbling out incoherently. At the threat of all the furniture ending up at the dump, the van time was rapidly changed.

By mid-afternoon her flat felt safe.

Returning to work on the Tuesday was a nightmare, she was jumpy and skittish all day. Carla knew how easily accidents could occur.

CARLA

It proved impossible to face the dangers of the office on Wednesday. At 9.30am, a surly voice jangled onto her ansaphone, pointedly demanding her whereabouts. The recycle bin at the bottom of the flats was an easy place to lose it, en route to the Doctors.

Carla didn't feel ill, knew she wasn't ill, but obviously needed a sick note. She feigned a bad back. Unconditional paid time was hers.

A week passed where she successfully squashed any fleeting visions of the accident. But on one afternoon that led into the night, she papier-mâchéd, to roundness, all the kitchen and bathroom edges. She crawled into her bed with the dawn chorus. Tired as she was, sleep would not come.

She was in Camden by 9.00am, waiting for the specialist bed shop to open. Carla purchased a round waterbed on her credit card for guaranteed next day delivery, persuading them to take away her square, double-sprung mattress.

The unfamiliar vibrations and movements of her new bed caused another sleepless night for Carla. Her ceaseless imagination began to examine other furniture in her home. The razor sharp springs of the sofa and the scythe edges of the fish tank danced in her mind. Pulling a sweater over her nightie, she dug out the telephone number of Help the Aged, ready for the following morning, to rid the flat of sofa and chairs.

She caught her fifteen fish, laid them on a sheet of newspaper, and apologising to each one, hammered their heads with her shoe. She rolled them up in the newspaper, sellotaped it over and over and squeezed the bulky parcel into the swing top. Finding a bucket, Carla then syphoned out the twenty-four gallons from her tank.

Eradications became more frequent, with a minimum of a few items each day, and with each eradication, Carla felt momentarily safer and in control.

Habitually, another layer of sellotape was wound around the filthy plaster each day, the festering appendage of her finger grotesque and misshapen.

Her rooms contained the barest requirements. The lounge housed a carpet and curtains, until the hooks screamed their dangers. The bedroom held the round waterbed and a heap of clothes, the hangers long since removed.

The kitchen had empty round-edged cupboards. No jars, no bottles, no crockery, no cutlery, just uneven papier-mâché edges curving the swing top bin, the washing machine, the oven and the fridge freezer.

Carla talked to herself, it made her feel safer to speak her thoughts out loud. Each time the accident began to mushroom in her mind, she began singing mindless tunes from childhood.

She was lying on the lounge floor, fiddling with the sellotape edges of her covered finger, when the reality of the sharp corners of the tape threw her into a new panic. She would have to papier-mâché them at once. But she had no paper to make the gluey mixture. She couldn't permit newspapers back into the flat, not with those dangerous words. She shook and wept, sinking to the ground clutching her knees, keening, rocking backwards and forwards.

Hours passed and her distress escalated until her mind exploded with the images she fought to escape. She sank back and allowed herself to remember.

Scummy froth hissing and bubbling beginning to seep over the lip of the pan, spitting onto the hob. Momentarily, Carla's concentration wavering from her task. Leaning over, turning the heat down, grasping the little brown-handled knife more firmly in her hand, she bent once more to slice the red pepper.

Before the knife touched the taut vegetable skin, Carla felt an urge to place the steely blade against her finger. She gazed at the picture, steel against flesh, then deliberately sliced into her body. Without pause to ponder, she raised the knife and sliced a parallel cut to the first and then another. Her skin turned stark white. The cut so deep it didn't bleed. It looked precise, orderly, fish gills on her finger. The image made her smile.

CARLA

She placed the knife gently on the chopping board and began to manipulate the gills as though they were gasping for air. She felt delighted by the simplicity of the image – until the cuts began to flow. She dabbed at the deep red blood ferociously and ineffectively with kitchen roll. The tip of her finger numbed, she felt no pain as the crimson fluid spread into the bubbles of the tissue in a jagged, irregular sea.

The cuts refilled swiftly after each dab. White gills, alive, red gills dying.

The blood began to flow more quickly, a small rivulet running down her finger. A crimson drop suddenly plopped onto the chopping board, a perfect round circle. Carla moved her hand, the next drop fell an inch to the right of the first. She repeated the action again and again. She marvelled that her blood could create such symmetry and beauty. A path of bloody stepping stones marched towards the half chopped red pepper. She squeezed her finger, the blood flowed more swiftly, the drops forming a tiny pool in the belly of the pepper. She paused and then with deliberation raised the pepper to her mouth, tipping it at right angles, allowing the sparse blood to trickle into her mouth.

'I'm eating myself.'

A wild animal scream ripped from her throat.

The harsh sound ruptured the madness of her actions. Carla began to quiver with confusion and fear. All the colours and images that had fought to the outside of her head were ensnared, wrenched back into their strong box and battened down, down into the dark labyrinths of her mind.

Gratefully, Carla felt her finger begin to throb insistently. She hurriedly threw the pepper into the bin, the chopping board and knife into the washing-up bowl.

Mentally shaking herself back to good old, dependable Carla, she went to the bathroom to find a plaster.

The Male Writer's Curse

by
Andrew

I'm not quite at this character's stage yet and I'm still hoping that underwear will be removed at some indeterminate time in the future, and that I will be there to bear witness.

His sexuality was fleeing at speed, heading south over Antarctic wastes. Soon, it would reach the pole, then it would be all over. No flag raising, no return journey. Just frozen wasteland from there on in. The huskies that were pulling his libido on a sled were going faster now, barking wildly as the load lightened. No barking for him. His dog days were done.

The mirror mournfully regarded him. Suit, once colourful, now grey. Hair, once proud, now defeated. Eyes, once alluring, now watery.

A lustful look would never settle on him again. Underwear would not be removed in his presence. Giggles would become prehistoric. Fluid would dry at source. A new ice age would begin.

At last, he thought, he could start his novel without distraction.

Tawdry Baubles

by
Janet

I used to be part of Crouch End Writers Group in London.
We set ourselves an exercise one week, five hundred words on
Christmas decorations. The themes were wild and varied. This
was mine.

She peered out onto the smouldering bonfire, warm now, snug
inside the house on the raw January day, her hands thawing
around her coffee mug. She watched the lazy plume meander
upwards. It hadn't really caught, too damp she supposed. She
pressed her forehead against the window and sighed. God
it was quiet, so bloody quiet. She'd probably made things
worse she realised because if it didn't burn properly, it would
still serve as a reminder, but a sadder one for its blackened
branches. The Christmas baubles lay intact around its base,
glimmering dully in the reflected grey light of the winter sky.

On impulse, she put down her mug, went into the
kitchen, slipped on her wellies, out through the back door
to the shed, pulled the rusty axe from its nails and ran
towards the bonfire. Here, she began to swing it wildly in
and around the Christmas tree.

She swung and smashed and cut, unaware of the snarls
emanating from her clenched jaws, or the tears spilling onto
her chest, or the tiny cuts caused by shards of glass that were
springing up with the destruction of each cheery bauble.

Such fury, such pain, such emptiness, such hurt, such
loss.

Twilight had tiptoed in before she quelled her mania.
A twilight that cloaked the nakedness of her emotion.

It was done, it was finished.

She slowly tottered back into the house, not bothering
with lights, crawled up the cottage stairs, stripped and slid

in between icy cold sheets. Then she lay numbly, incapable of pushing memories aside. Now beyond tears, beyond rationale, her mind filled with cruel pictures and thoughts.

His face, unfamiliar after forty-six years, sitting across the breakfast table, revealing to her his plans for the rest of his earthly life; his plans that did not, could not include her. He was sorry, but yes he was leaving her. She, the mother of his four children, the wife who had supported and cooked for endless dinner parties throughout his career, the wife who'd put her life on hold to help him climb to the top of his ladder. The stupid foolish wife who had embraced his retirement as time for themselves, of loving and adventure. No, no, there was no one else, but surely she could see how they had grown apart? Surely, surely she could see how she had stopped growing long since? Why hadn't she gone back to work? His leaving was surely the best thing for both of them.

He ensured he engineered one last family Christmas with children and grandchildren. And it was on Boxing Day, as they sat alone over toast and marmalade, he calmly destroyed her life. He spoke, he left and all by lunchtime.

There would be no more Christmases; after all, there were no more baubles to dress a tree.

DIY-Oh

By
Andrew

This is coming. In my lifetime. No doubt. But then again, I was wrong about the solar powered fingernail clippers.

The Death Squad arrived an hour late. Traffic. They squeezed into his sad but expensive little flat and crowded round the recliner. The doctor perched on the arm of the sofa showing shapely calves and a concerned bedside manner. Aaron noticed the calves and filed them away as something he used to be interested in, but now had no opinion on. The police officer stood at rest with hands clasped over genitals and smelling of secret cigarettes. The social worker couldn't settle, even though there was room for two on the leather sofa. And the lawyer was all hippy and made himself at home cross-legged on the floor. Not wise thought Aaron. He hadn't vacuumed for over a year.

"Why do you want to die, Mr Fischer?" asked the doctor.

One cursory glance to take in both the state of him and the flat should easily have answered the question. But he knew they needed him to say something. The social worker had a GoPro camera strapped to her chest. She pointed it towards him expectantly.

"Wouldn't you? If you were me?" said Aaron.

The footage would show, if anyone ever cared to watch, a messy room with curtains drawn against the optimistic sun. A once high-end brown leather recliner containing a puffy pale faced straggly bearded overweight middle-aged man, exuding an aura of hopelessness that was clearly visible to anyone except the most hard-hearted fellow human. In easy reach of surprisingly slender fingers sat a low table containing evidence of a life less lived. Takeaway boxes, beer cans, a nearly empty bottle of Laphroaig single malt clinking next to a solitary clean glass, and the TV remote.

"We do need you to be a little more specific, I'm afraid. As part of the decision making process, we need you to state your exact reasons for wanting to, er, proceed."

The lawyer smiled as if he was on a beach being handed a cocktail.

"And, er, to the camera, if you would." Another big smile and a nod to the chest, as if willing Aaron to nobly raise his head and deliver words of such Shakespearean dignity and emotion, that they would leave all assembled speechless and tearful.

"I've just been, you know, depressed. I mean, what's the point?"

"Have you been taking your anti-depressants?" enquired the doctor. "Because we can always up the dose, or try some different ones?"

"No! I said I wanted to die and that's what I want to do. It's my right isn't it?"

"Well, yes, subject to certain checks and balances to determine the exactitude of your situation and to ensure that there is no coercion by any third party or parties," beamed the lawyer.

"No one wanting you dead for the money, is what he means, sir," announced the policeman, fingers twitching in suppressed desperation for future nicotine.

"No. No, there's no money."

A short awkward silence, then: "Perhaps we could hear your original application statement, sir, for the record, and you'll have a chance to add to it or make amendments." The police officer nodded to the social worker, who, multi-tasking admirably, pulled out a phone and started reading, while simultaneously chest caming the glowing text.

"My name is Aaron Fischer," she read, "and this is my request for Life Termination Pharmaceuticals under the Death In Your Own Home initiative. I've had depression since my job as a Life Insurance Actuary was replaced by an algorithm. I tried to get other work appropriate to my skills and qualifications but those jobs are all gone. I obtained casual work in a distribution warehouse on about ten percent of my previous wage but was replaced by a drone that could scan boxes sixty-eight times faster than me. Then my girlfriend left, then I was knocked down in the street by some teenagers and I twisted my spine and I'm in constant pain. So I want to go and I understand I meet the legal requirements."

"Anything you want to add or has anything changed since you made your request?" grinned the lawyer.

"Savings nearly all gone now," mumbled Aaron.

"Duly noted for the camera," replied the social worker.

"Very good," chirped the lawyer. "So all that remains are some formalities concerning your last will and testament, which as you will know will super-cede any previous will and cannot be legally changed or amended for six months from the date of this visit, as per the Serenity Act of 2024. Let's get that sorted now, shall we?"

Aaron nodded.

"So, any living relatives you would like to make a bequest to?"

"My brother. Australia. No Christmas card. So fuck him."

"Probably just lost in the post, Mr Fischer," soothed the doctor.

Aaron didn't bother to look up.

"The good news, Mr Fischer," said the lawyer, "is that the government is prepared to make a contribution towards any person, organisation or charity of your choice, based on future savings to society. Now a lot of people we visit have a bit of a struggle understanding this, but I'm sure that with your actuarial expertise, you'll have no trouble getting up to speed with the figures. Sally, if you would?"

The social worker read from her phone once more.

"So Mr Fischer, you're 47, your expected life span is 92. By going before your 48th birthday, or the 5th April, whichever is sooner, you'll be saving society 44 years in benefits and state pensions, plus a notional amount calculated based on a human footprint assessment; for example use of iNHS, power, water, refuse, internet use energy, CO_2 emitted, possible future use of emergency services and so on. Our assessment of your case determines a saving to society of £968,432.37, and we will make a donation to a person, charity or incorporated organisation of your choice of 20% of that amount if you so wish. Do you have a person, charity, or incorporated organisation you'd like this money bequeathed to Mr Fischer?"

"No, no, I don't. Can't you understand? I just don't care anymore."

Things limped on like this for quite a while as the functionaries carried out their legal duties. Aaron just wanted them gone, to get the drugs, and be done with it. Finally, after a few subtle nods between the team, the lawyer piped up once more.

"Well Mr Fischer, excellent news, you've been approved. The DIY-Oh package will come by courier within the next forty-eight hours. You'll just need to sign for it. There's full instructions inside and, of course, a helpful YouTube link so you can see the best way of setting it all up. Is there anything else we can help you with?"

Aaron shook his head at this bizarre question, then watched the team pack themselves up and leave, with a breezy "Cheerio" from the lawyer and rather more appropriate somber looks from the others.

As the door closed behind them, he realised it had been the largest number of people who'd ever been in his flat at the same time. He felt an urge to run to the door and offer them all a drink. Later, sipping a large whiskey, he wondered if he could somehow turn this around. Maybe it wasn't too late. He could try those exercises the eGP had suggested for back pain. He could just see the back stretcher device peeking out from behind the sofa, neglected and used just the once. He could get up and go for a walk, maybe the teenagers would have moved on by now. He could even visit a coffee shop! Make some plans!

A few whiskies later Aaron drifted off in his recliner. Sometimes, he found a position where his back pain wasn't too severe. The painkillers did work but also brought him out in a rash and gave him dark thoughts. As he twitched and grunted in semi-sleep, he wondered if he should do this thing. Could do this thing. He couldn't see a way out of his pain, his uselessness, his hopelessness. But a tiny bit of him said he should go on, that things would turn a corner, that something amazing would happen, that tomorrow was another day, the first day of the rest of his life. Then, a deeper sleep took him for once, and a dream of sunny beaches and shapely calves entered his thoughts. He woke in the early hours feeling more optimistic, then drifted off again, possibilities in his mind.

A loud ring woke him and he sat up too quickly in shock, twisting his back painfully as he did so. His swearing was interrupted by the ringing again, the doorbell, but this time the bell push was held down for, well, an unreasonable amount of time. What was this? Fire? A glance at the clock said 07.12. Who the hell? Still groggy, he heaved himself off the recliner, and made it to the living room door before leaning against it, heart pumping with the sudden exercise and back screaming. Then the doorbell rang again three times, followed by an urgent banging.

"What the fuck!" he shouted. "Just wait, I'm coming!"

He shuffled the final five steps to the front door and yanking it open, saw the back of a yellow Hi-Viz jacket heading away fast down the corridor.

"Hello?"

The croak was just loud enough for Hi-Viz to hear. It was a burly courier, who along with the orange, wore cargo shorts and Timberland boots. Aaron had once owned a pair of Timberlands another lifetime ago.

Hi-Viz did a one eighty and marched back, a small box in his hands. Aaron didn't notice how wound up the other man was. Social interaction had never been his forte at the best of times, but under normal circumstances his first word could be interpreted as friendly.

"Timberland," pointed Aaron.

Hi-Viz ignored the boot brand opener.

"Do you think I got all day waiting for twats like you to answer the fucking door?"

"But," Aaron mumbled in shock, "it's seven twelve."

"Yes it's late and I've delivered fifteen packages already and there's another hundred and fifty to go, and," he added, taking in Aaron, "if everyone was a sad slow cunt like you my day wouldn't finish till tomorrow."

"How dare you!" but Aaron was washed away by the wave of pissed off white van energy.

"I get to my depot at five fucking a.m. so cunts like you, who lie in all day, can get your precious fucking useless packages. So take this, put your pinky on the reader and fuck off back to sleep."

The package was thrust into Aaron's chest and the finger reader slammed on top. No one had been in his personal space like this for years. He fumbled his finger onto the device, it beeped and was snatched back.

"If I have another shit day like this I'm just gonna DIY-Oh for a bit of fucking peace."

Hi-Viz turned on his heels.

Aaron finally got up to speed.

"Well, that's what this is."

The boots spun round. Hi-Viz grabbed the box and sure enough, there was the iNHS logo and a warning note about Pharmaceutical Products To Be Kept Away From Children printed on the label.

"That'll teach him," thought Aaron as he waited for a reaction and an apology. But British society had clearly moved on since Aaron's isolation. Hi-Viz suddenly began to laugh, making a nasty throaty groaty sound.

"Yay! You've made my fucking day! Ha! Fucking Brilliant. Go on, in you go, take the drugs and fuck off. One less useless lazy cunt in the world!"

He pushed the box back into Aaron's chest, and still laughing like a blocked drain, made his way back down the corridor.

Aaron finally came up with a response.

"Yeah, fuck you too, I'll get you the sack you, you cunt!"

"Yeah, you go for it Timberland." Distant now and out of sight. "I'll have yer boots!"

The awful laughter finally vanished behind the block security door.

Now furious, Aaron filled with a sense of purpose.

"I'll show 'em, I'll fucking show all of them!"

Back pain forgotten and feeling furious, he rushed back into his kitchen, groped in the drawer by the sink and found a never used vegetable paring knife and wildly stabbed open the packet. Bits of cardboard and polystyrene flew everywhere.

"Bastards, bastards, I'll show 'em, fuckers," he yelled, as the instruction sheet fluttered to the floor. There were two mini yoghurt-sized bottles; one blue, one red. The red had a skull and crossbones printed on the side. He rammed down the childproof top, twisted it off, threw it in the sink, yanked away the silver foil and drank the lot. His mouth filled with an outrageously bitter taste. He bent over, retched, tried to draw some water, felt dizzy, picked up the blue bottle, saw the words "Sweet Strawberry Flavour Sedation & Mouth Preparation," and felt his knees go. Aaron tried to hold onto the sink, missed and fell to the floor, hitting his head on the drawer handle on the way down. He tried to say something to nobody, tried to breathe, spasmed, twitched, twitched again, and that was that.

Karma - A Fable

by
Janet

So many women are raped and don't report it. I want those men to pay for their violence, and not always with a prison sentence.

He's forty-five, but an old forty-five, do you know what I mean? Of course, you don't know him as well as I do. I've known him almost thirty years. I go with him everywhere, I'm one of his prize possessions. One of the only things that he really owns. I'm saddened when I see him now, but then, he led himself to this place, single-handedly. He could have changed his path of destiny, but he was too... too what? Stupid? No, never that. Uncaring? Arrogant? Foolish? It's hard to sum up his life in one word.

Of course, he thinks life has treated him unfairly. Although even there I could be wrong, the last two months have seen a change in him. His eyes when he looks into mine seem haunted, troubled. He read an article in *The Sunday Mirror* a few months ago about Karma. He read it twice. 'Bloody hell,' he said out loud to himself in his bedsit. 'Bloody hell, that can't be true or I'm fucked!'

I've travelled with him to many places. I have no judgement on where we land, although this place is probably the grottiest. He's tried to make the best of it. Or did, he seems to be letting things slide recently. I was his second project in woodwork. I'm not fancy or inlaid, but I'm a basic and hard wearing mirror. He was good at woodwork, he liked the feel of the different woods, he was expert with the plane, stroking, teasing me into a surface of silk. Even received a certificate for me, the only certificate he ever received. He was as pleased as punch. But at fifteen, he left school and didn't pursue his obvious skill.

He drifted from job to job, girlfriend to girlfriend. He had many of each, love 'em and leave 'em. He was good with the chat, which helped with both. And he was in a gang of four, they trod the dance-boards together, hunting for women. He was successful, he was small, cute, eyes a-dazzle and he could dance and flirt magnificently. He should have received certificates for those as well. But, of course, he didn't.

The gang of four were inseparable. They vowed they'd be friends forever. In their teens this seemed like a reality. They all had nicknames, names created to describe their pulling styles. Rum, Cheetah, Twinks and Bugs. Rum said with two double rum and cokes inside them, they were a guaranteed lay. Cheetah was a skinflint and would wait until they were drunk at their own expense then pounce on them, they rarely refused his advances. Twinks would use his eyes to flirt and then his toes to dance them into bed. Lastly Bugs, who would put plastic spiders in girl's glasses, and when they screamed, go to the bar on their behalf and get them a free drink. What he actually did was remove the bug, add a little spiked coke or lemonade and wait for the girls to feel the effects before laying them wherever they fell.

They had no scruples. They notched their lays upon a chart that Rum kept in his bedroom. It was a very competitive sport for them that took up all their free time. When they reached twenty, the jobs weren't so easy to come by. They moved en masse to London and began to work as builders. They lived in a house in Hendon. It was cheap and it was ugly, but it suited four bachelors out for a good time.

Things began to change between them. Bugs ended up in hospital, beaten by a bouncer who didn't like the idea of spiked drinks being given to unsuspecting females. Bugs was shaken, the punches to his head affected his balance and his confidence, so he went home to the safety of his mum. That left three and three isn't a good number for a gang; it means two can side against one. But the relentless competition for bedding women went on and on.

One night, Twinks came home, he was shaking and supercharged, I thought he'd succumbed to drugs. But no, not in the sense that I assumed; he had succumbed to a drug of his own making, adrenalin and power. He looked at me, preening and peacocking at himself all the while. I've been a very, very naughty boy, he said and laughed. He didn't say what he had done, but he seemed pleased with himself. Whatever it was, he didn't tell the others either.

Cheetah met a girl who took his heart. He broke the rules of the gang and started dating her. It put a further strain on the household. Sometimes, she would be there cooking, taking over the kitchen, nagging them about the dishes. Rum made a pass at her after an unsuccessful night. A fight ensued and Cheetah moved out to live with her. Twinks and Rum and I moved to a smaller place. They were beginning to feel afraid, so they pretended they were invincible to each other. The competition rules still applied.

It was here that Twinks displayed the odd behaviour of before, posturing and posing in front of me. This time he couldn't help but boast and told Rum all about it. 'It was so easy,' he said, 'she played right into my hands. I danced with her all night, on and off. Followed her around, she had the choice, she was a cock teaser. She brought it on herself. If she'd just said she would come back here, or if she took me back to her place, but no, she was asking for it, flirty cow. What gets me,' he said, 'is why are they're surprised when you have to force them? They know they've been asking for it, sending out the signals. This one, she wouldn't accept it, kept talking. Bitch. She soon shut up, one good belt round the gob. In, out, shake it all about. She was dry though, I hate that, specially as I knew she'd been turned on all night. Bet the bitch did that on purpose. And then, like the gentleman I am, I got up, helped her up too and apologised that I'd got carried away 'cos she was so beautiful. Then I called a cab. I even arranged to meet her tomorrow night. Silly mare believed me. I could see it in her eyes. How could Cheetah have been sucked in by a woman?'

Both men discussed the point at length. The competition rules changed after that. They never came home without scoring, it's just that sometimes the women needed a little more persuasion. They were clever. If they apologised afterwards, the women seemed confused and did not scream out and did not tell. At least that's what happened for a while, until Rum picked an older woman who did report it. The police came to the flat but Twinks was there alone. Both men packed their bags and moved north, where they could lose themselves in the home town they knew so well.

And of course, as nature intended, they calmed down a little and met and married and slowly their ties of friendship loosened and they lost touch with one another. Pieces of gossip would circulate. Cheetah's mum died of cancer. Bugs got done for shoplifting. Little snippets of this or that.

Twinks married a small woman he could dominate. He went to night school and trained to be a cabinet-maker. He got a good job and began to receive respect from those around him. He went up in the world, buying a semi and filling it with beautiful things. After all he had the eye. She gave him two lovely daughters, beautiful and blonde. And as the girls grew into adolescence, his nightmares began. He went to the doctor to say he couldn't sleep but the sleeping pills couldn't stop the dreams.

The girls started going to discos. Twinks was in terror. If anyone, anyone did anything to his girls. But then how would he know, how could he protect them? His sleeplessness made him irascible. The family home was full of arguments. He ended up hitting the woman he could dominate because he didn't know what else to do. His beautiful daughters were furious and flew to her defence. His wife was terrified. The next time he hit her, the daughters told him to leave until he could sort himself out. He rang Rum after a space of seven years. Rum no longer lived where he had been, and Twinks could not trace him. Bugs was inside again, another petty crime, and Cheetah never returned from London. Twinks was alone.

But his wife loved him in a fashion. She tried to help him help himself, but he was too afraid to see someone about his problem. He knew there was no solution. After all this time, he could not admit his thirteen rapes. All past and buried, he had thought. Ten months ago his wife told him she'd met someone else. Twinks was destroyed. He had not realised how or when she had become his mainstay. The following week he discovered his sixteen year old was pregnant and was going to keep the baby, the father was unknown. Did that mean she was raped against her will? Or a cock teaser? Or worse, she knew what she was doing? His world moved further away from him.

And it was from that point, he began to age and became an old forty-five with a potbelly and weary slouch. Now his looking into me is a horror. The lines, the greyness, but most of all, his eyes only see his blackened soul. His taste of hell is now.

The Rapture

by
Andrew

In 2012, I got tickets for the London Olympics. Entering the stadium I was overwhelmed by the sheer number of people and the hum of excited voices. And I also have this DVD called 'Life After People' which imagines a world where everyone... just leaves. And it shows how quickly the natural world re-asserts itself. Combine these two random thoughts with my love of sci-fi and out popped this story.

Mick lay in his hospital bed trying hard to feel some pain through the drugs. He knew he shouldn't fight it but he hated the haze, the uncertainty of what was real and what was a dream. He hoped the screaming parts were dreams although he really couldn't tell. In a semi-lucid moment he tried to pull out the lines but the machines went mad. An angry doctor came and yelled.

Later, the fat nurse with the haunted eyes sat with him. He definitely felt someone holding his hand.

"Not long now," he thought she whispered. "Not long till what?" he wondered, and then he was off again, into another world that seemed familiar, but how could it make sense? He dreamed of, or was it remembered, a fight in a house – not his house in London, but a strange foreign house – of shooting a gun, his gun, at men, and when he could shoot no more, using his bayonet to stab and cut. Then, somehow, Linda came in to ask him if he wanted a cuppa, and he was in his London flat drinking tea and watching his wife slowly slip her nightdress over her head and tease him from the end of the bed. Then the killing would start again and he would be cutting, stabbing.

One day, he woke from a dream, or memory, of a nearly dead cat in a dusty street asking him again with a pleading stare if he wanted a cuppa, only to find an ugly weasel face looking closely into his.

"Linda, Linda, Linda!" shouted the weasel. "I'm fuckin' sick of hearing 'bout Linda you fuckin' dipshit!"

Suddenly awake, he instinctively went for his bayonet. It was always on his left side, but when his hand reached his hip, all he could feel was jelly. He pulled it back in revulsion.

"Oh, now you fuckin wake up, you ugly mufucker. Maybe now we'll all get a little peace. You ain't the only one hurt. Dipshit!"

Another American voice. "Easy man, easy." More awake than he'd been for a long time, he could see a battered looking young man in a wheelchair tugging at the weasel.

"Don't fuckin' touch me, cripple."

As the weasel stomped away, Mick noticed both his arms ended in jellied stumps. Wheelchair man maneuvered himself nearer the bed.

"You been out a long time, man."

"Texas," whispered Mick, remembering the accent of the man in front of him from hundreds of movies.

"Yeah man, Houston, spot on. Hey, I'll come and read to you later."

"Read?" said Mick.

"Yeah, I'll read to you. We all need to prepare. Won't be long now."

"What won't be long?" asked Mick, but the wheelchair was off, leaving him to take in his surroundings properly for the first time. He was in something that was a cross between a bed and a tray. A blue jelly like substance covered most of his left side, although his ankle and foot poked out at the bottom, looking unharmed and incongruous against the blue ooze. His right side was covered with a plastic blanket, and underneath he could see inputs and outputs coming and going. With an effort he moved his hand to where the jelly met his skin. It wobbled slightly but he couldn't get his fingernail under it, the jelly seemed to be part of him. As he poked, he felt an old sensation. He couldn't place it for a moment and then remembered: pain.

He only had a moment to savour this before wheelchair man was back.

"You must have been in Medina, right?"

Medina. He remembered. They had been laying siege to the holy city when the orders came through to withdraw. They were going to nuke it, after all. His unit hadn't made it far enough away. He remembered a blinding light, then agony, then nothing until now.

"Is it over?" asked Mick.

"Naw, not yet. Will be soon though. They're all starting to leave. Just a few fanatics still fighting on."

"Leave? Leave where?"

"Man, you have been out a long time. People all over leaving. Ain't nothing the army can do 'bout it. So hush now and listen."

Mick watched the wheelman open up a well-thumbed Bible and begin to read.

"For the Lord himself will descend from heaven with a shout, with the voice of an Archangel, and with the trumpet of God. And the dead in Christ will rise first. Then we who are alive and remain shall be caught up together with them in the clouds to meet the Lord in the air."

Mick tried to stop him.

"Hey. Wait. I'm not a religious man. Stop."

"Don't matter. As long as you ain't a Muslim, you're comin up with us. And…"

He broke off suddenly and wheeled away. Mick noticed the fat nurse approaching with a cheery looking doctor. Noticing Mick's rebirth, the nurse came over with her half smile. "Not long now," she whispered.

"Attention everyone," called the doctor. Another yank. "I know y'all can't wait to get the hell out of here. Or perhaps I should say the heaven outta here." A groan from the assembly. Clearly, Mick had missed a few visits. "The army is bringing you all home ASAP, before everything falls apart. Lots of people have gone stateside now. We want to get you all back to your families so that you can leave together. I know some of you aren't quite fixed yet but time is of the, you know, and anyway, it won't matter once you leave. I imagine you'll all be fixed up good when you get to where we're all going."

A ragged cheer. "So, we'll get you all de-blued for medevac in the next 24. And don't worry," he said, noticing Mick. "We'll be going via the UK, so we'll drop you off somewhere nice."

Over the next few hours the meds disconnected the ward. When Mick's turn came, they sprayed him with a toxic smelling fluid. The blue went gooey, then sloughed off. Nurse scraped it away with what looked like a chef's spatula. He tried to ask her about what was going on but she shushed him and mumbled psalms under her breath. And besides, the pain was exquisite. When all the blue was gone and the lines out, his burnt and blistered wounds were revealed in all their glory. In places, scabs came away in chunks, revealing delicate baby skin below. Terrible cramp came when he tried to move but when that passed everything seemed to work, just about.

The wounded soldiers made a macabre procession out of the ward, shuffling or wheeling past rows of beds containing mostly blue mass; technicians were pulling lines out, not to healing but to a twitch – and then nothing.

"Poor bastards," said Mick to Houston.

"No man – they're lucky – they'll already be where we're heading." His eyes went dreamy. "And the dead from all times were resurrected and reunited with whom they had lost in the endless plains of Jericho." Mick didn't engage with this. He just wanted to get back to London, hold Linda, and have a cup of tea. Maybe then everything would be all right again.

Two days later, after hours of waiting in disembarkation areas, moving in overcrowded military trucks and a scary flight in a huge C-5 Galaxy, he finally landed at Northolt, west of London. He said goodbye to some of the Marines he'd been able to talk to over the noise of the flight and was finally able to piece together what the hell had happened in the two months he'd been out blue.

It seemed that shortly after the war went tactical nuke, people across the world started to have visions, epiphanies, messages from God or whoever, telling them to gather together with family, friends and neighbours and prepare for the Rapture. Apparently, this was also happening to the other side. The crazy jihadists were getting it too. So were the Hindus, the Buddhists, the Shinto people, the Jews; in fact, just about everybody. Even the secularists and those who believed in animal spirits had got caught up in the idea that something better, something wonderful, something... heavenly was waiting, just the other side of the rainbow.

Then people started disappearing. The first to go had been some of the small Amish communities in the US. The authorities found neat wooden settlements just tidied away. In the biggest barn, piles of clothes had fallen limply, and there was absolutely no sign of the people – like a mass suicide, but with no bodies. Then, the Mormons started leaving messages and videos and Facebook posts saying they were going to meet their God. The police and media found cameras left filming nothing. But when they were rewound back, the cameras showed scenes of praying, mass hysteria, mass joy, images of intense bliss. Then, there was a soft pop, leaving an empty room, and the clothes people had been wearing slowly settling to the ground.

The governments and big business hated it, of course. They had a war to fight and money to make. But within a few days everyone on the planet with an Internet connection or a TV had seen the answer to all their problems. The war, climate change, poverty, injustice, sadness, pain. Within a few weeks, the US evangelicals had been filling football stadiums to capacity. Preachers found it easy to tap into the visions that now pretty much everyone was getting. And the planet was emptying out.

Mick's journey back into central London was desperately slow. The trains seemed to have stopped and the buses were worse than Sunday service. In the hours it took him to get back to Islington, Mick could only think of one thing – Linda. The yanks said they'd sent her a message to say he was alive and coming home. He hoped beyond hope she'd got it, that she was still home, that she hadn't vanished with a slight pop to who knows where, and that she had the kettle on. Once he could see Linda, hold her tight, smell her soft body and hear her dirty laugh, he could begin to find his bearings again.

The bus stopped far sooner than it always used to. He tried to argue with the driver about it, but just got that weird "won't be much longer" shrug he was already starting to hate. He had to walk the last two miles, wincing in pain as his new skin and wasted muscles struggled to get back to somewhere near normal. The streets were quiet, shops closed, and traffic light. Uncollected rubbish blew around. The few people on the streets were closed in on themselves, although he did see a pack of kids throwing stones at a supermarket plate glass and shrieking like wild animals as each window shattered. The sight and sound of life cheered him, but his mind always reverted back to Linda, Linda.

Finally, finally, his heart pounding with exertion and anxiety, he reached the block of flats where they had shared their years of love and drinking. Trudging up the stairs, he hesitated at their front door, hoping beyond hope that she was there. There was definitely someone inside. Loud music, like a choir, reverberated through the door. Loud music was definitely Linda, but gospel music? No way. Linda was more RnB.

There was five minutes of banging and ringing before the door opened and Linda's warm and curvy shape appeared, a vision to a lost soul.

"Mick! Praise Jesus! You're just in time."

Before he could say a word, she pulled him through the door and hugged him tight. He dared to breathe. All too soon the hug was over. Linda looked him up and down with bright eyes.

"Tea?"

"Fuck yeah."

He followed her into the small kitchen. Things were not right. The place was spotless, so unlike Linda's usual chaos. And it was like she was high on something. But apart from vodka, Linda had never been a druggie. The kettle clicked off and Linda handed him a chipped mug.

"What's this?"

"Tea."

"It's green. And where's the milk?"

"Oh Mick, don't worry about that now. We've got to be pure for tomorrow."

"What?"

"At the old Olympic stadium. Two o'clock. We're going to leave all this behind."

"Linda. Baby. Stop, stop. I'm not going anywhere."

"Mick we have to go. Everyone I know already has. We'll be taken into heaven."

Linda went all glassy. Mick noticed that she had a small book dangling from a chain around her neck. She reached for this now.

"And the believers and those pure of spirit will be gathered up and released from their earthly concerns in a great noise."

"Come on Linda! What the hell? Where's all this come from? You're not religious, you hate churches. Greedy hypocrites, you used to call them. And you'd tell the Jehovah's Witnesses to go fuck themselves when they came round. Even the children. And…"

"Yes Mick. I was a sinner. But God forgives. And you've been away forever. Things have changed. We have to go. And we can start again. In heaven. You, me… and Jesus."

He just stood there, at a loss, holding the steaming mug of insipid green something, warm at least, in his cupped hands. Linda reached for a spray gun and began cleaning the already pristine work surface.

"Pure and clean Mick. We must be pure and clean. We can't be left behind."

It went on like this for a long time. Mick sat on the sofa, exhausted and afraid. Several times he tried to pull her near to him, to hold her, touch her, make love to her. But each time she pulled away. Not pure she said. It was like all the Linda had been sucked out and replaced with nonsense. But what could he do? She told him he was a lost lamb, and he supposed he was.

The first time he'd been in the stadium in 2012, he'd been lucky enough to get tickets for the 10,000 metres final. The sheer number of people, and the electric happy energy of the multitudes had blown him away. Today, if anything it was more crowded. All the seats, the newer football area, the track, the grass, all full. He tried to guess the numbers. 150,000? At one end was a podium, almost too far away for Mick to see. TV screens showed a diverse group of vicars, priests, African preachers, Pentecostals and evangelicals; plus, bizarrely, what looked like all the aldermen of the City of London, wearing their finest golden chains.

Mick looked around at the faces nearby. Some were already in an advanced state of ecstasy, others were crying, some agitated, some holding children tight as if in a last embrace. He looked at Linda, who was already at 6 on the E scale, mumbling meaningless silent words, eyes open but seeing God knows what. He tried to reach her hand but it was stuck like glue to the little book around her neck.

Huge screens all around showed recordings from similar stadiums, people praying and screaming to God, then vanishing as one.

A priest in purple robes came on the PA, his voice filling the stadium. The crowd softened to an expectant hush.

"Here we are. At last. The happiest day of our lives, the day we never believed would come." Mick didn't feel happy at all. "And now, two thousand years after Jesus Christ, our Father in Heaven, in his wisdom, is bringing us, his children, his poor lambs, back into the fold for his infinite blessing."

It went on like this for some time. Mick didn't feel part of it. He'd seen so much killing and death. He couldn't feel joy. He couldn't actually imagine that he was going to some crazy place that he didn't even believe in. But maybe he would. Maybe he would stand before God, who would judge him for all the terrible things he'd done.

The call and response began, then the chanting, faster now. He looked at Linda. She'd never seemed so far away.

She was the only thing he wanted. Not this. He shouted her name. Somehow, she heard him above the din. Her eyes blazed at him.

"Mick! What the fuck is your problem! Focus! Or I'll leave you here. Is that what you want?"

For just that second, there was the old Linda. Difficult, angry, lovely. Then she was back into her chant, eyes tight shut, surrounded by her old Linda wall, plus something else, unreachable.

Mick began to panic. He tried to focus, to be in the zone, to say the words projected onto the huge screens. But this was all wrong. The crowd was in a frenzy now, the drumming and chanting even louder, plus another noise, a whirring and a smell of static electricity. He felt his hair begin to fizz with charge and a vibration in his teeth. One of his fillings disintegrated and his mouth filled with nasty blackness. And then suddenly, all the noise stopped, a great pop, and stillness. He looked around for Linda but she had gone. Her clothes were settling on the floor, the little neck book falling onto them with a soft plop as he watched. Gasping, he looked wildly around, not believing. The stadium was empty. A small fire had started near the banks of speakers. As he looked closer, he saw others, not many, maybe a few dozen, looking around, stunned. On the podium, one of the Aldermen was weeping silently, all the priests around him had vanished.

In a daze, he bent down to pick up Linda's clothes, as if she might somehow be underneath them, as if this was all a silly trick. But nothing, no hole in the ground he could walk down to reach her. He brought her jacket to his nose, smelling the last of her perfume. He sat down and began to wail.

The next few days were a blur. He'd been back to the flat, but couldn't stand to be there. So he'd broken into an empty house for sleep. In the days, he'd wandered aimlessly through the mostly empty city. At night, he listened to the few radio stations still broadcasting. TV and Internet was over. Things had gone right back to basics. The BBC was still putting out one FM station, and searching round the waves he found calls to the next stadium events. Plus a few crazies on the pirate stations. Power was intermittent, shops closed. His army training had kicked in and he was now eating from tins stolen from abandoned supermarkets. He didn't much care though if he lived or died. There didn't seem to be much point in carrying on now, after the war and Linda going. The words Post Traumatic Stress rolled around in his head, not really connecting.

One evening, ten days post-Linda, he broke into a posh tower block and made his way to the roof. He sat on the parapet wall, feet dangling, not sure whether to jump or give it just one more day. As he sat, and as the sun set, he was treated to the most beautiful meteor shower. All points in the sky were lit up by shooting stars. He'd never seen anything like it in his life. As the sky calmed him, he climbed off the parapet and lay down on the roof, gazing up at the sight. Maybe this was a present from God, he thought. Maybe all those who had left were right. And now it was the end of the world. Well, that would be all right by him, he thought as he drifted off to sleep.

Next morning, woken by bright sunshine, he felt much better. And hungry. That had to be a good sign. He switched on his little transistor radio for company.

"…one with military training report to Trafalgar Square ASAP. Unidentified flying vehicles and ground craft reported, using unknown energy weapons on anyone moving."

Then, there was another voice, BBC sounding.

"Last night, astronomers in Chile and France trained their optical telescopes on low Earth orbit to find the reason for the unprecedented meteor showers. They were shocked to see huge clumps of what appear to be human bodies up to 300 miles out, being drawn into the high atmosphere and burning up as they re-entered. Unconfirmed speculation is that these are the bodies of those somehow displaced from stadiums and other mass events, drawn into space using technology as yet unknown. This clearance of most of the population seems to be the precursor for the attacks taking place today."

Mick had heard enough. The bastards. Bastards! His hand went for his missing bayonet. Remembering. He would get a new one. And take his revenge. For Linda.

Astraphobia

By
Andrew

Have I been to more than two hundred dating events? Probably. They're even more painful now I'm getting older. Oh well. Maybe this story helps balance things a little.

He hated speed dating but it was that or another lonely night in. Dating was much more difficult once you reached your mid-fifties, although he hadn't enjoyed it much in his thirties either. And the facilitator tonight blew an annoying whistle every five minutes to tell the men to swap tables. They were on round five now and the damned thing had made him jump each time.

He wasn't really listening to Dawn or whatever her name was. There had been no attraction, no spark with any of the women so far. He'd scanned the room at the start and realised he didn't actually fancy anybody there at all. This was an over-fifties speed dating event. Why were men in their fifties doomed to be attracted to women twenty years younger? The curse of the normal middle-aged man, he supposed. As Dawn talked on he began a fantasy about Aristotle Onassis, and how an older wealthy man such as him would be able to attract young beautiful women and invite them to his yacht whenever he wanted. He then began a secondary fantasy that interrupted the first. Merely thinking about Aristotle Onassis dated him horribly. No man in his twenties would ever even...

"So that's what Astraphobia is," said Dawn.

A short silence and his default nice man mode kicked in. "Sorry?"

"That was a test to see if you were listening," said Dawn, looking at him directly.

"I was," he lied.

"So how would you define Astraphobia exactly?" Dawn sat back and folded her arms.

"OK, I wasn't listening. I'm sorry. I'm being a shit."

"Try at least and guess what it is."

"Astraphobia?"

"Astraphobia."

"Err, Astraphobia. A fear of being hit by an asteroid?"

"Not bad. Fear of being struck by lightning. It happened to me, but I didn't die."

"Really? God!"

His interest aroused, he leaned back into the conversation and noticed that, in fact, Dawn had lovely black eyes and a calmness behind them that he suddenly found appealing.

"Did it change how you thought about dying?" he asked.

"Oh, now that's the best question I've had all night," whispered Dawn, meeting his gaze and unfolding her arms.

The whistle blew and Dave spilled a bit of his wine. Dawn's giggle drew him in and he smiled for the first time that evening. Maybe speed dating could be OK after all.

Sheet Lightning

by
Andrew

*A short nonsense poem to accompany the previous story.
It seemed apt.*

Sheet Lightning strikes me on the Head,
It makes me Dead,
I wish I'd stayed in Bed,
Or sheltered in a Shed
Instead.

At least now I'm Dead,
I won't have to steal any more Lead.

I never was any good at it anyway.

Say Cheese

by
Janet

Oh, I love the idea of people's karma biting them on the bum!

His pomposity is settling around the dinner table like a malignant odour. His conversation is peppered with the staccato gunfire of I, I, I, I, I. My wife has seated him at the head of the table, her new guest of honour. Little does the poor man know his future. I think his means of conversation reflect perfectly the miserly proportions of his skeletal frame. Extraordinary hands though, huge and bony, fingernails long and pared of any dirt. He wheezes a laugh frequently, falsely frequently. The sound is reminiscent of dry wind on a desert whipping sand into eddies of sharpened particles of glass. I wonder what his secret will be? Gillian, my wife, will expose it to the table if she thinks it right. Or not and keep us all hanging with bated breath.

I loathe Gillian. Let me try to remember when my loathing first began. There, throughout the six years of our tortuous marriage certainly. And there, tangible on our wedding day. Oh, I had tried everything to escape that day, but her game-players mind was always three steps ahead of mine.

I glance at her now, posing her crystal beauty, porcelain skin; her dress a sheath of silver fabric, accentuating the contours of her perfect body. My wife, charismatic, charming and so cruel.

Conversations are droning on around me. There's I, I, I, I, I from the top end, and flutter murmurings from Sally on my left and Rachel on my right. But my wife has taught me duplicity. Here I sit at the dinner table chewing, listening, conversing. Here I am in my real self, sitting back and observing and plotting. Oh so endlessly, fruitlessly plotting, but so many of my well-laid plans have been thwarted. I can only assume that Gillian has a power beyond my human perceptions.

Eight around the table tonight. All Gillian's toys. All, as I am, secretly awaiting Gregor's shaming. To feel his supercilious superiority disintegrate as Gillian unfurls his misdemeanor, petal by petal, course by course. It's happened to us all. And Gillian is so adept. The first two or three gentle, hinting disclosures to be mistakes, perhaps a mere misunderstanding of the confidentiality she had enticed us each to believe in. But then the deliberateness of her divulging becomes unmistakable, her enjoyment apparent and your capture assured. And within a meal you become a tiny mouse to her predatory cat, an assured playmate as long as she desires you to be so. As long as she allows you to be so.

We are all successful people, all in various ways within the public eye, all monied. But Gillian's game in life is not for mere wealth, although her joy in accumulation is close to her only passion. No, my wife has craved, does crave, and will always crave ultimate power.

'Darling,' the softest bark of a command, 'more champagne.' Mark and I both reach for the bottle. A momentary hiccup, poor chap, he'll pay for that. At dinner parties I am always Darling, in her bed it could be anybody. At present, and for the last six months, it has been Mark. Although I believe everyone around her table has been forced through her bed. Her appetite is insatiable and sadistic.

The importance Gregor attaches to his work is implicit in his conversation.

'Of course, a man of my position, I hold a lot of responsibility...'

'Of course, a man of my position, I have the answers that people want...'

'Of course, a man of my position, guarding such treasures, you can imagine, I'm always in demand.'

He has come to take on the characteristics of his job – a fusty, bony relic of a museum curator. But the curse of the pyramids is about to descend upon him, poor man.

Sally has drunk too much wine; lately, she always seems to be drinking too much wine. Drunkenness angers Gillian and I see her glance at Sally. Last time she crushed her swiftly with words of splintering ice; this time she's decided to leave Sally unharmed. She's turning her attention back to her guest.

'Cheese and biscuits, Gregor?' she enquires sweetly.

'I don't mind if I do,' he bares his teeth, an imitation of a smile, or it maybe his attempt to flirt with my wife. Difficult to tell.

The cheese board is passed along the table. He inspects the fine display and blanches. I didn't see anything amiss with the cheese board. I crane forward, slightly, as I don't want Gillian to see my curiosity. No, I can still see nothing amiss. But he is greatly perturbed and I can see a smile of malicious pleasure on my wife's lips. He raises his eyes to hers.

'Pretty, isn't it?' she says.

He nods. She lets us in on the secret. 'The cheese cutter, it's of a rather,' she pauses, 'special design.'

'Oh, can I see it?' pipes up Sally, trying to be helpful, trying to ingratiate, trying to be right.

'Shut up!' Sally tries to disappear.

'Where did you come across it?' manages Gregor.

'You know.'

'How could I possibly?'

'Why silly, it's from your collection.' The still silence is like a fog.

'Is it?' he stumbles, he is not a good actor.

'Well, you sold it, remember?'

Gregor leaps up, 'How dare you,' he blusters, just as we all had done. 'Are you accusing me of…'

I don't listen to his words, Gillian always researches her subjects thoroughly. Instead, I watch his angular body twitching in agitation, his neck mottling with red. His movement magnified by our static stillness. We all watch. He runs out of words, so he runs for the door instead, which as we all know is locked. He tries it three times, the eternal rule of comedy.

'I'm not accusing you, no, no. I know you sold it.'

'This is outrageous!'

'I even know to whom you sold it.'

'Liar!'

Gillian's eyes narrow almost imperceptibly. 'Cheese and biscuits anyone?' she purrs.

We know the procedure, carry on as though nothing has happened. Cut him out, cut him dead. The conversation again picks up to a murmuring momentum.

'No more wine for Sally,' Gillian says gaily.

'No, no had enough now, actually.'

'Yes, you have. I think we should have a lovely game of charades later, don't you?'

With sinking spirits we all agree wholeheartedly. Charades is a game that Gillian uses to expertly humiliate us. Gregor stands on the outside of the pleasantries, insecure, angry and exposed. He stays there through the cheese and biscuits, the charades, the fruit, the holiday conversation, the coffee and mints and, eventually, joins us for the vintage port, sinking into his chair defeated.

'Ah, Gregor, so nice of you to rejoin us,' Gillian says without looking up. 'Now do you want to tell everybody what you've been up to or shall I?'

He starts again, pushing his chair back and over, then says loudly: 'What…'

I want him to hurry up and tell us, for I wish this endless evening to be over.

'Gregor has been a very naughty boy,' begins Gillian playfully, 'a very naughty and a very greedy boy, haven't you?' She doesn't wait for a reply. 'Gregor's found a way to improve his finances, but in a somewhat unorthodox manner.'

Gregor's face now hosts the inhuman colour of purple and is beginning to glint with sweat.

'But Gregor has put himself in a very silly and a very vulnerable situation. Let's face it, if little me knows about his misdemeanours, well, it begs the question, who else?' The last is said with a baby-girl voice as Gillian sweeps our faces with glittering eyes, the lioness before the kill.

And the poisonous dart of the question hangs in the air for an age. We had all been hoisted by the same hoax at our initiations, and so we don't leap forward to rescue Gregor with words. Too selfish I suppose, too happy to see someone else suffer at the witch's hands.

'Now, unfortunately Gregor, I've let the cat out of the bag and we all know about the innocuous little cheese knife.' Her hand elegantly glides over us, the guests, the 'we all'. And then in a sultry whisper adds: 'And just between friends obviously, the same supplier informed me of one or two other treasures that have gone amiss in his magnificent Museum.' Her gaze rests upon her prey. 'But Gregor's latest exploit is beyond imagining.' The tinkle of her laugh.

Gregor's mouth is open but he does not speak.

'Shall you tell them, or shall I?' There's the tiniest of pauses before she continues, 'Oh you spoilsport. From what my sources tell me, Gregor has begun to revel in the clandestine meetings of the criminal fraternity. Naturally, this applies only to the masters of their trades.'

Gregor is trembling.

'And now,' she carries on relentlessly, 'he has met with Philippe Jardeneau, have you heard of him?' We shake our heads. 'An art forger of excellence.'

Gregor is panting.

'Philippe, such a charming man, is on his third attempt to faithfully recreate the single sphinx from the Pyramid of Djoser. I am right, aren't I, Gregor?'

Gregor explodes.

I see a whirlwind at the end of the table, I see the colour of cravat. I see the cheese knife protruding from the neck of Gillian. I cannot register what I am seeing. I cannot feel what my response should be. Gillian is leaning towards me imploringly and there's just the cleanest trickle of blood jagging downward from the blade. But neat and perfect as Gillian is, the exquisite handle looks beautiful against her pale skin. I'm a little bemused. Her eyes are beginning to bulge, what she is trying to say with them I cannot fathom, even though they are staring straight into mine. Movement and sound appear to be suspended.

Gregor is standing a step behind my wife. He looks perplexed. He stabbed the evilness from Gillian with one stroke. He's not purple anymore but a shade of snow-slush. Sally whimpers like a puppy. It jolts me. Gregor is murdering my wife. Has murdered my wife, she is just taking a while to cease living. I start to laugh heartily. I see the angry pain in her eyes at my amusement before she shudders once and collapses rigidly against her chair. We all, bar Gregor, begin to laugh and laugh.

Gregor's eyes are wide with terror; at her revelation or his action, I can't tell. Of his revelation, I have no judgment, of his killing of my wife, I feel pure joy. I have a nudging at the back of my mind. A nudging to escape. I glance around the table and realise we are all of a same mind. As a body we rise giggling and swamp around Gregor, who has given us our freedom, returned our souls, released us back into society.

Someone, it wasn't me, has removed the weapon from Gillian's neck and now we use it to steal the life of the man who has unlocked our destinies. This man doesn't know of our secrets, our desires for acquirement. How we have all broken the commandments of life. This man doesn't know that we have all been Gillian's bedfellows, that we have played court to her for the retention of our greedy needs: financial, carnal, slothful and perverted. And he cannot know and because of this, we cannot let him live and we need to assuage our wasted years.

Gregor acquiesces to our onslaught silently. We stab him and stab him with rising hilarity, releasing our bonds and years of frustration.

He's dead. She's dead. The atmosphere is lighter.

'My car's the biggest,' says Sally soberly, 'they'll both fit.'

'Where?' says Richard breathlessly.

'The quarry?' I'm saying.

With tacit agreement, we lay the bodies on the lace tablecloth and begin our laughter soaked heaving towards the locked door.

Lewisham High Street

by
Andrew

The real plaque is still there, but I don't think anyone sees it anymore. You can stand in a place where there was once a huge explosion. Sometimes, I do just that when I go to M&S to buy my pants.

It wasn't much changed since the same day last year. He leaned unsteadily on the arm of his great niece and surveyed the view. The uninspiring 1960s high street, tarted up by colourful tacky shop fittings, except for Marks and Spencer with its tinted glass and automatic doors. The market was still there, busy with fruit and veg alongside large-sized blue tartan laundry bags and packs of 48 AA batteries of dubious energy levels. That was him now, he supposed. The people weren't really much different to those from 1944. Solid working class, mostly poor, cheap clothes. One thing was different. How did people get so big? There were people everywhere, happy and sad, downtrodden or wearing the arrogance of the young and the macho. Probably no one here would believe the energies unleashed at this spot all those years ago. There was certainly no trace of it now. But embedded in the pavement, the lonely plaque was still there, often trod upon but rarely read.

The words were the same as always. "On Thursday 28th July 1944, fifty-one people were killed when a V1 flying bomb landed here."

Simple words that couldn't sum up the scene that he witnessed when he'd arrived ten minutes later looking for Maisy. The whole front of Marks had just gone, the back of the building suddenly visible and nude through the dust. A great hole had opened up in the pavement, big enough for a bus. Of Masons fish stall there was no sign. His mother would be cross with him when he came home empty-handed, he thought in a daze. Broken glass was everywhere, glinting in the sun, and there was a sharp hiss as water bubbled out of pipes that didn't usually see the light of day. At his feet there was a human finger with a neatly manicured nail, lying gently on a background of brickwork, as if it had been arranged for an exhibition. He could see that finger even now in some part of his mind. Crying and moaning surrounded him alongside the organising shouts of the ARP. Of Maisy and many others, never a trace was found. Completely vapourised someone said later. He wondered if there was still a tiny speck of Maisy dust hiding in the structures of what was here now. Enough. He didn't want his great niece to see him cry. He took a sideways look at her but there was no danger. She was doing something on the device she always carried with her, a far away look in her eyes and her lips slightly parted in a fugue-like state. Perhaps he could reach Maisy on this device, he thought for a second. Sentimental old fool he said angrily under his breath. He squeezed the arm of his great niece to indicate his annual pilgrimage was done. What was her name again? And how did she get so big?

Gravia's Dreams

by
Janet

Here's a second idea that came to me on holiday in Vietnam with my sister. I became fascinated by the TV channel dedicated to the harsh life of people fighting for survival in the Yukon. It started me thinking about potential Yukon money-making schemes… Note to self: must go on holiday adventures more often!

More sodding day tourists! Gravia slapped on her Yukon scowl welcome, glad her father wasn't there to reprimand her. Without looking, she expertly caught the rope that her brother threw to her and heaving, pulled the small craft alongside the jetty and secured it tight.

Eight Americans from Georgia – four men and four simpering women, all her grandparents' age – but, as was typical, all dressed too young. All babbling in a breathy Georgia twang:

'Oh my, this is soo exciting!'

'Hold my hand Bill, I'm afraid of slippin'!'

'Marjorie, careful, careful honey!'

Gravia stared out at them from her square Yukon face atop her squat, strong Yukon body. She shunted the walkway into place and held out her hand, grunting at the nearest tourist and yanked her on land. Her brother snickered.

'Oh my, this young woman is so strong!' yelped the wrinkled bag, giving a breathless giggle.

Gravia hated the tourists, did everything to get out of showing them around. But Papa was not one to be disobeyed, especially as the government had cut the salmon window to eighteen measly hours. How was any decent, hard-working Yukon family to over-winter on that? Two years ago, here in Teslin, it was four weeks fishing. So Papa decreed they had to diversify and opened the house to tourists for two hours every Monday, Wednesday and Friday, June thru to August.

Moose hunting, bear hunting, even wolverine hunting had to be better than tourists.

The women were all too thin and brittle, sporting pastel coloured skiwear and ludicrous green sun visors. Two towered over Gravia and two were just a little taller than her. Gravia was a typical Yukon – sturdy, bulky, solid, amongst her contemporaries, she was considered good stock and 'pretty'. But Gravia had a different view of herself now, having to mix with the tourists.

They made her angry and jealous in turn. She envied the paint on their faces, the delicate designs at their ears and necks, the fact they always seemed to have a husband to oversee their well-being and safety.

In Yukon, a woman had to prove her value by bringing home the meat for the family, skinning the wild animals they shot and making good practical use of the fur and the leather.

Yukon women didn't have time for fripperies. The seal oil they used on their faces was necessary to protect from frostbite, and really didn't smell so good, especially as the winter progressed. But these women always smelled like the rare spring flowers at the beginning of the thaw.

She pushed her way past the tourists and started tramping towards the homestead, shouting a guttural: 'Come,' to the excited explorers.

She loathed showing them around the house, as they delicately poked and exclaimed and commented with face, eyes and voices. It had made Gravia look at her own life with dissatisfaction.

'Oh Bill, no pictures… anywhere.'

Why would they have pictures in their homes? You couldn't eat them, they'd only give momentary heat on the fire.

'Clive honey,' one of them whispered, 'do you see any mirrors?'

'I do not Cindy, not a one.' This was also spoken sotto voce.

Mirrors? The tin by the door, were they blind?

So, after the third invasion, Gravia decided she needed something back and began to pilfer. Only little tiny things they probably wouldn't miss, but things that gave her an expanding view of the world outside her harsh environment. To begin with, it was only things accidentally dropped in the boat. However, Gravia discovered that by pushing into them as they tried to pass her she could delve into pockets and open bags and increase her treasures.

The first thing she took was a red tube of something. It felt slick, oily. Seal oil? She'd rubbed it over her face, it felt nice, it even smelt nice. More surprisingly it tasted nice and sweet, like a fruit. It was her first unwitting encounter with cherry lip balm.

The second thing was a tiny, weeny little gold leather bag; bigger than a purse, but not like the handbags she'd seen in magazines. She worked out it would fit half a dozen of the red tubes, but nothing more, which made it a pretty useless object in her reckoning. But she took it and hid it under her mattress anyway.

The third thing was completely pointless – a dainty pair of satiny gloves in turquoise blue, with three pearl buttons that fastened at the wrist. Well, obviously not Gravia's wrist, as her stolid hand became stuck at the opening of the gloves. No amount of wriggling allowed her to reach the finger parts. And they were far too light and thin for Yukon weather. Why had the woman brought them with her? Clara, the owner, kicked up a hell of stink when she couldn't find them and pulled in everyone to search the boat high and low. But they were safely stuffed down the back of Gravia's pants to be viewed later.

From there on in, having the tourists became a secret game. Gravia almost, but only almost, began to look forward to their arrival, just to see what little things she could ferret away.

In between tourist visits, Yukon life still had to go on and Gravia was of an age where she needed to find a mate, as her father repeatedly reminded her. She was coming to an age when he couldn't afford for her to be his sole responsibility. She had to choose a mate who would fit her family and increase their chances of survival in the depths of winter. A strong Yukon man who could stalk, shoot and build.

Gravia had her eye on Ethan. She'd met him at the previous summer meet. He was big and that made her feel small; he was strong and that made her feel protected; he was monosyllabic and that made her feel sophisticated and chatty. And Gravia felt that Ethan had his eye on her. He seemed to be beside, beyond or behind her for the whole time she was there.

On the shooting range, he applauded her high scores – along, she admitted, with many others, but Ethan stood out to her. In the timed 'skinning the marabou' competition she won her usual first and couldn't help but notice Ethan in her eye-line. He never looked at her directly but he was always there. And, of course, she knew his bravery from the usual small town gossip. He'd shot his first bear at only fourteen and rescued a friend who fell through the ice.

They didn't communicate with word or eye contact, but Gravia felt their proximity at the meet spoke volumes. This years' meet was due in three weeks. Gravia had already decided to use the slick oily stuff on her face and neck as the smell was so pleasing, and Ethan too might be reminded of the scent of spring flowers.

But between now and then, she had nine further tourist visits to endure.

A group of English ones, their accents like splintering ice, didn't like to be touched and rarely smiled. Valerie yielded a tiny lacy handkerchief with the initials VB embroidered in one corner. Stupid, you'd only be able to use it once before it would be full. Megan lost a silver filigree necklace when it slipped to the bottom of the boat, which quickly made its way to the bottom of Gravia's jacket pocket. Too tight for Gravia's thick neck, but a treasure all the same.

From other tourist visits, she collected one of the ubiquitous green visors, a mobile phone and a silver toothpick.

The week prior to the meet, one of the 'little things' was a delicate, slight young man. He was travelling alone, squished into the boat between six of the older tourists. His big blue eyes were framed by pale lashes, his blonde hair wispy and unkempt. Gravia was entranced. She pulled him out of the boat last, holding his hand slightly longer than was needed.

He smiled at her shyly, murmuring: 'Thanks.'

Gravia thought he was the cutest thing she'd ever seen. She had an overwhelming desire to cosset him, protect him. Unlike the other tourists, he came into the homestead, leaned against a wall and simply looked. He didn't touch anything, comment on anything, just looked. And Gravia, inexperienced in the ways of men, just looked at him.

She wanted to steal him and put him under her mattress but, of course, she knew that was ridiculous, he'd suffocate. But Plan B would work, she thought.

As she led the party towards the privy – why they always got so excited about seeing the privy, Gravia would never know – she ensured that the young man was at the back of the line. Being the last to poke his head through the privy door, he was also last in line to troop to the next amazing sight, to gawp at the idle salmon wheel, allowing Gravia to deftly trip him up. She felt cruel doing so, but it was the only way she knew to keep him for a while.

Slight as he was he fell swiftly with no time to break his fall, hitting the hard ground face first. Gravia was kindness itself as she swooped to pick him up, roughly shoving her sleeve under his bleeding nose.

'Alright?' she said.

The slight one couldn't speak as her sleeve was in the way, and he was hurting. He thought his teeth might be broken and he had a phobia about blood. He would have slithered to the ground again if Gravia wasn't holding him up with her other arm.

The twittery tourists had all rushed back, with little cries of 'ohh', 'ow', 'ouch'.

'You alright, Vernon?'

'Vernon,' said Gravia, trying it out for size.

'Here Vernon,' another twanged, passing him a tissue and forcing Gravia to remove her arm from under his nose.

'What happened?'

'He tripped,' Gravia stated. 'As he turned round.'

'Did I?' Vernon muffled.

'Must have done,' Gravia said quickly.

'I guess so,' the slight one affirmed.

The tissue woman again, 'Your nose is bleeding so much, is it broken?'

'I don't rightly know.'

Gravia made a sudden movement, bringing her eyes level with his nose. 'It might be broken.'

'Oh my,' the plumpest woman said, 'Should we call out a doctor or something?'

Gravia snorted with laughter: 'Not out here. We fix ourselves.'

The tourists were a-twitter with concern. 'Oh, gosh,' 'Oh, golly,' 'Oh, my!' They were incapable of coming up with a plan. Gravia took the lead, rounding them up like sharp-tailed grouse before she shot them for the cooking pot.

She called on her brother to continue the tour down to the river while she took Vernon to the homestead, keeping a tight grip on his arm, afraid her new treasure might try to fly away.

She sat him at one of the mismatching table chairs, shoving a grubby tea towel against his nose to stop the flow of blood and fetched hot water. It wasn't broken she assured him, just a nosebleed, as she jabbed at him with a dishcloth soaked in household disinfectant. He squealed loudly, taking Gravia by surprise. She sat back, eyes wide.

'Owwww,' he moaned.

'It's only a nosebleed!'

'It really stings,' he snivelled.

'It will, but not for long.' She lunged at him again. He swerved violently and fell off his chair. Gravia was perplexed: 'This will stop infection!'

He lay whimpering on the floor. Gravia shot out a hand to grab his jacket to pick him up. He screamed; 'No, don't touch me!' And burst into tears.

Crying was not something familiar to the Yukon race. And a man crying was just not done. Gravia watched Vernon with fascination as tears streaked across his face. He didn't even try to wipe them away.

Gravia realised this 'little treasure' was a wimp, not worth putting under her mattress, even if it did kill him. She carried on watching him dispassionately from above until his sobs hiccupped into silence.

'Your nose is still bleeding,' she observed.

He pulled himself upright, gingerly settling into his seat. Gravia pushed the bowl and dishcloth towards him; wimps could sort themselves out.

Nodding, Gravia made her decision. Ethan was the man for her, she'd tell him next week. They could get hitched before the fall.

The Journey
Of My Death

(A Lament for a Friend)

by
Janet

This is a true story.

The tortuous journey towards my death is a story to be told. Not to be enjoyed once in its written form, but because it needs to be told by me, the future corpse. Before my illness, I never thought of dying. Death yes, but never dying, and when the child doctor nervously gave me his four-month prognosis, I had no understanding of the arduous course he had prescribed for me.

I remember wishing passionately that he would die, so the words would remain unsaid, and I could lie in my clinical bed, my only worry the buzzing of the kamikaze bluebottle hurtling around my room.

I had requested to see the doctor alone; my actions were construed by others as being brave, but far from it. My actions prevented the indignity of relatives weeping and holding my hand in theirs, or worse, my tears and their pointless comfort.

'Four to six months,' he said.

'Why don't we say five then?' I countered. He reddened, but stood his ground, his back pushed hard against the sticky vinyl of the utilitarian hospital chair.

I was surprised, I knew I was ill, I knew the chemo had left me weaker than before, but I didn't feel any iller than I had before. And here this young man was forecasting my death. I felt the five long year fight in my heart begin its slow ooze.

I didn't cry, I railed. Four to six months, my, what could I do? Cash in my policies, go skiing, scuba-diving, bungee jumping? Four to six months, I'd see Christmas in then. One more sumptuous Christmas dinner with all the trimmings, so what?

I asked him to leave, but called him back when his hand reached for the door.

'How will I die?' He looked perplexed. 'Not eventually, between now and then, what should I… look out for?'

'Look out for?' his brow furrowed in confusion or was it distaste? I didn't care.

'What will happen to me physically as my body succumbs to the cancer?'

'Do you want me to talk to you now?'

'Do you want to wait for four to six months?'

'Wouldn't you like someone with you?'

'You'll be with me.'

He faltered, his excuses having run dry and began to move back towards the chair. I almost felt sorry for him, but only almost. My sorries I needed to hoard for myself.

His second line of defence failed too as I sensed him hiding behind his medical jargon. I came out on the attack, using my intellect against his unease, crashing through the safety barriers medical school had taught him, fighting for truth in language as clear as a bell-jar. But I quieted as his relentless list extended.

I clarified an initial point. 'The growth will eventually be pressing on a nerve?'

A faint inclination of his head.

'And that will prevent my legs from functioning?'

'No, no, not quite,' he searched the ceiling for his words. 'The causal pain when the growth presses on the nerve will necessitate an epidural to ease it.'

'The epidural will take away the use of my legs?'

'Yes, yes, in essence.'

'Yes or no?'

'Yes.'

A safety line, 'Do I have to have the epidural?'

'You'd be more... comfortable.'

'But I don't have to?'

He shrugged and gave an apologetic half smile. At that moment, I didn't understand the wealth of his knowledge. The catalogue continued at my insistence. Further hair loss, double and dimming vision, loss of appetite, continual nausea, heightened susceptibility to infections, likelihood of complications due to secondary growths, colostomy...

'Colostomy?' I spat.

'As you lose the feeling in your lower body.'

'Only if I have the epidural.'

'Yes, only if you have the epidural.'

'Well, I'm not, and I repeat, I am not having a colostomy bag!'

'It's not as difficult as patients assume.'

'It's not the difficulty, it's the indignity! I'm forty-one for God's sake!'

'Ah,' he floundered, as I heaped my human emotion of vanity upon him. We sat in a sticky silence for a time.

'What else?'

'Are you sure you want to...'

''I haven't lost my mind yet, go on, what else?'

'You'd probably like to know that ultimately it won't be the cancer that kills you.' I resist a ripe retort. His eyes widen in horror at his faux pas and I enjoy his subsequent struggle to repair. 'I mean, that you die from, ultimately, eventually.' He runs out of steam swiftly.

In a voice of syrup, I ask: 'Oh, what will I ultimately die from then?'

His eyes in his very pink face now cannot connect with mine. He's desperate for an escape but he battles on and wins a brownie point for doing so. 'Your kidneys, as the treatment progresses."

'Treatment?'

'Yes,' he misses the irony. 'The huge toll on the kidneys due to the drugs, well, er, it will get to a stage where they will be unable to cope.' His words are beginning to tumble from him, no longer measured in their patient explanation. 'They will cease to be able to cleanse the body, leaving it ostensibly drenched in poisons.'

I push him further whilst my voice remains strong. 'And will I be lucid to the end?'

'Unlikely, the kidneys failing will cause immense tiredness and sleepiness.'

'Sleepiness?'

'Slightly heavier than a sleep.'

'Coma?'

'Probably a state in between.'

I digest this whilst staring wide-eyed at the very plain cream wall opposite my bed.

'I'm not going to leave here now, am I?'

'Unlikely.'

'Am I?' I pushed.

He stuck to his guns. 'Unlikely.'

'Thank you, you can go now.'

'Do you want to…'

'No, nothing, now go and close the door behind you.'

He did and without hesitation.

I sat in my bed too tight to cry. So this room was to be my first tomb. But in five months, my tomb would be a tiny box that would snugly fit my five foot five frame. I wonder how many times within this room, going across the whole width, stacked floor to ceiling, the little tomb would fit inside this massive tomb? Don't know, I'd have to ask for the measurements of the room and then, of course, the measurements of the average coffin. I'd get my partner to bring in my calculator, as I'd never do it in my head. I'd better get him to bring in my accounts as well, work out my figures, get everything shipshape. Don't want to be a burden before or after my death. So yes, my accounts, I should make a list, my insurance policies, check everything is up to date. And my diaries, I need to destroy those myself, far too many secrets of a life led. I'll have to rip them page by page, I won't be able to burn them in here. Could I trust my partner to do that without looking at them first? Reverse it, what would I do? I'd read them, I know I would. So no, I'd have to destroy them, no point tempting fate. And why hurt him now, the one affair was a dalliance not a fixture. Like me, a dalliance not a fixture. The tears came from a reservoir deep in my being and somehow navigated around the growth.

* * *

Three to five months to go. To go before I die, I mean, or to put it another way, a month from the diagnosis of my time on Earth. I have suffered a month of torture. They call it depression, I call it realisation. Then they allocated me a Counsellor. Jim, I think he's called. He comes and sits in my room for one hour every other day, we haven't really spoken. I wish he wouldn't come. I don't want to 'come to terms' with my forthcoming death, it doesn't give me pleasure. But he persists, that's his job, it's what he's paid for and maybe I'm considered to be a challenging case that he can discuss in his T-break with his healthy colleagues.

The nurses have said that I've been much nicer to treat the last few days. I hadn't been aware that there was a protocol of manners of how one should approach one's premature death. Small talk does not trip easily from my tongue at this time of my life. My growing helplessness ignites my anger. Why can't they understand that? I am prisoner to my illness and a prisoner to their timetables and moods.

I used to wash my hair every day, here they wash it once a week. Such a simple thing has crushed me on certain days when I look at my flattened strands in the mirror.

I used to be so energetic; here, there and everywhere, rushing, laughing, dancing, running. Now I'm hoarding my energy to myself and my steel will. My most energetic choice all day and every day is whether I can stand the pain a little longer or whether I'm going to succumb to drugs that dull my thoughts and close my lids in a tidal wave of exhaustion. It is a difficult and unpleasant choice and when I have made it, I always seem to question it again and again.

My partner has suffered, I see the anxiety through the joie de vivre he tries to bring into my sick room, death room, every visit. He's still bucking against the truth, keeps bringing in articles about new cures – shark tablets this morning. It's laughable but I'm too miserable to share the joke. It's tiring, his endless optimism on my behalf. I need him to share my acceptance that the real fight is over. The cancer has beaten me and I have no more reserves left to deal with treatments that would require boundless hope to start upon them. Yes, that's the word to describe my state, hopeless. I don't want him to feel hopeless too, but I need him, so desperately, on my side.

Family have been dutiful, travelling the long distance each weekend, wasting hours at my bedside, no doubt remembering the same ritual with mum only two short years ago. I'm glad she died before me, she would have found this difficult.

And friends, who are more hesitant about how to broach the subject. 'I'm so sorry...' What am I meant to reply? 'Me too.' I've sharply challenged one or two. One I've frightened away forever. I have no time to be nice anymore, only truthful. And if they decide not to mention my death, I find I cannot talk to them at all, for that too is untruthful.

One huge change in me, I no longer have names for people. I categorise them, as friend, partner, parent, doctor, nurse, counsellor, ghoul. I don't have the wherewithal to care emotionally about all the different factions, but if I label them, I can come up with the appropriate conversational style and it uses less compartments in my head.

* * *

12th December, two to four months, lucky me. Two months, December and January have thirty-one days, two extra days, but then February plays the joker! Win some, lose some. Continuous mind games with myself. Maths and quizzes and mazes and flights of fantasy inside my mind. And no one knows as the drugs and I have perfected a look of glazed simplicity whilst emotions rage and pupate so closely under the surface.

My mind picks up the humour and word play of visitors, but it takes an age for my eyes and mouth to register my enjoyment, by which time they have whisked onto newsy-news, worthy-news. The lack of response to their jests makes them feel they must be misplaced. And I, well, I don't attempt humorous delivery now. My thoughts from my mind to my mouth take centuries of time and my punchy punchlines lose their power.

I must be slow, slower than I think, because visitors keep leaping to my aid, to reach for the cup, to steady it at my lips, to help me comb my scraggy locks. How I wish they'd leave me to my tiny daily triumphs over myself, minute victories over the creeping decay of my limbs.

My legs stopped on, oh, a few days ago. My colostomy bag drips quietly, an exhalation rather than a drip, hidden under ugly pyjamas, wynsyette for warmth. Me, the queen of exotic silks and satins, of sheens and shines and wefts and weaves. A smile curves in my mind as I recall the Indian markets, fabrics whispering in the breeze, glorious colours vying for attention.

I wake every morning, ready for a new day, until I remember and weep to wakefulness to another long and painful morning till snooze-time at two, two hours of oblivion, of pain-free flying in my mind.

Today, I had a visitor written on my timetable; friend she's called. Due at twelve, not twelve-twenty, as it is now. Always late, even at my speedy dying, she's late. How selfish, but latecomers are selfish, tied up in their own world of petty problems, not thinking of others, of me. Sand in the egg timer running out, running out, second by second. Two to four months and she's late.

I sat myself in my oh-so high-tech wheelchair for her arrival. The chair supports my tired neck, holds steady my weary arms. Soft, padded and padded seat to stop bedsores, bum sores. Can't stop the heart sores though. And I can hide my ugly lumpy legs under a chequered blanket. Vanity, in my condition!

She came eventually, fifty minutes late. I gave her ten of mine and sent her on her way. I feel swamped by my pettiness. She got lost, she claims.

'No *A to Z*?' I queried, tartly.

She apologised, but then she always did. She was surprised at my anger, I was surprised at her gall. My time is precious, she should have respected that.

* * *

One to three months. Drugs are administered every four hours now, plus I have my intravenous personal morphine button. But that's monitored, so I can never give myself too much, never overdose. But for all the pain and discomfort, I don't want to overdose. I want to live, squeeze out every moment of my aliveness.

Euthanasia. There was a programme on the TV last night. My partner fled to switch it off. I held him still with my slow and slurred, 'Let's watch.'

He sat down defeated. We watched in silence, holding hands. At the end, I pierced him with a look.

'I don't believe in euthanasia.'

I needed to make my message clear as cut glass and I repeated slowly and laboriously: 'I don't believe in it!' But this slowness was due to the drugs, not my content.

The passionate outburst exhausted me and I fell into coma-sleep, happy in the knowledge that he had truly heard me.

On Tuesday, or it could have been Thursday, I woke feeling iller than ill. The doctor told me it was to be expected. My rage at his glibness and the feeble throwing of my water glass, encouraged him to take tests. I had pneumonia. More drugs, different drugs, and as my body closed in upon itself to mend, my eyes closed against outside distractions. I heard the doctor and my partner mutter over my soon to be dead body.

'This maybe for the best.'

'Yes.'

'She may just slip away.'

'Yes.'

'The pneumonia will strip her of any last vestige of energy.'

'I see.'

'I think you should prepare yourself.'

'Yes.' A choking sigh.

'She's fought so hard, this really could be for the best.'

Fury forces my eyelids apart. I glare from one to the other and slur: 'Not a corpse!'

They pull back stunned.

'Not being beaten by pneumonia!'

Immediately, I slide into an abyss of total fatigue, furious at my lack of staying power.

They acclaimed my recovery as astounding. Their conglomerate praise made me more nauseous than the drugs. One to three months, every single second is important.

* * *

Nought to two months. No days or sixty days. I could have life snatched away today. What shall I do to make it memorable? Just in case? I'm too endlessly exhausted to switch on imagination. My breathing hurts. I'm yellow, haggard. A ghoul of my former self.

So many scented potted plants and flowers from friends who are concerned and do not know what to do for the best. I wonder if they researched that smell is the last sense to go. I'm weak, so weak, every action is exhausting. I insist on trying, slurring and dribbling as I snap and snarl every single time a pair of hands leaps to my needy aid. The balance has swung, I cannot do things for myself. Quality of life, quality of dying.

* * *

I'm on borrowed time. Like a moth to the flame, I keep flickering to the surface of consciousness and overhear I have pneumonia again. Immune system is refusing to work with drugs. Kidneys have failed, poisons are stockpiling in body. Can't eat. Heard doctor say, I'm dangerously thin, strange sentiment.

Can't see, only light or dark. Can hear, can smell, can feel partner's hand enfolded over mine. Am in scary place of shadows, caverns, with no arrows to point the way. That's why I keep coming back. Am scared of this dying. I'm not religious but hedge my bets and manage to mumble for the last rites. Couldn't hear what priesty said, but felt his presence in the room.

Afterwards, I felt my partner's mouth against my ear.

'It's OK, you can leave, it's alright to go.'

Knew the effort that must have cost him. Need to thank him, have to hold on a little longer to thank him.

More time. Feel my partner reach inside my heart again. Now in the gloom I can see pinpricks. Pinpricks that beckon of adventures untold. I'm in limbo-land. Halfway, betwixt and between. Known and unknown. Pain and no pain? Fight back, back, back, my heaviness hindering my passage, open my eyes and look into the iris of my love.

'Yes, okay.'

He saw me, he heard me, he smiled tenderly. I saw the tremulous teardrops of love courageously held in check. He stroked my face, once. And then I let go, sank into myself and away.

Gatecrashed

by
Andrew

I went to a really bad party in a room atop a pub where I hardly knew anybody. I sat alone nursing a beer and wished for an adventure. Instead, this story arrived in my trousers.

The sign at the bottom of the pub stairs said private party. That had never stopped me. I stepped over the red rope and got into character. Flowing through the door and briskly into the room, I noticed a table with birthday gifts and cards. A dull looking woman in a brown jumper was passing a present to another lady, who, I reasoned, not unreasonably, was the birthday girl. Too dumpy for me. Four out of ten. I moved into a dark corner for surveillance. It was then I spied the bony blonde.

Settling into my spot against the wall, I watched her dance jerkily around the room and knew I wanted to fuck her. No one else was worth my attention. Social worker types and wispy arty men. I stared at her again. The dancing was bad. Maybe she'd drunk too much. That would be a plus. Short black sleeveless dress, matching high heels and that was it. Honey blonde and skinny. Soft, pretty face though. Maybe forty-five. I needed someone tonight. And she might just fit the bill.

I filtered my way through the other dancers, edging carefully past the birthday girl as she and two men flung themselves around an old Michael Jackson number, beer glasses in hand. Target directly ahead, and still alone. Talking wouldn't work here – too loud – so I used my direct approach. Taking blondie's hand and putting my other around her waist, I moved into tango mode and took control. Her eyes widened and she looked shocked but I leant in close and whispered: "Sexy", nearly biting her ear as I did so. She didn't pull away, so I took that as a good sign. Pulling her body closer and moving my waist hand down to control the tips of her buttocks, we spun around the room narrowly avoiding the dancing chaos surrounding us. As the track neared its end, I slowed and looked deep into her eyes. There was a trace of excitement there, her lips had parted and she was breathing heavily. Stopping her dead, I enfolded her top lip in mine and at the same time pulled her into my groin. I nibbled gently for a nano second, then severed all contact and stood away with a little bow. "Nice dance," I mouthed, turned and headed briskly for the bar. If she followed, my night would be sorted.

It was then that my plan went to rat shit. The bar was heaving and a lost youth was struggling with a dismal lager flow and till anxiety. These social workers, or whatever the hell they were, couldn't organise a fuck in a whorehouse. But you have to maintain momentum. I moved closer into the crush and made eye contact with the man standing next to me. "We'll die of thirst here, mate," I shouted. A nervous half smile came back with a mumbled yeah, but I had to keep it going. Never stand around like a dick.

"How do you know the birthday girl?" I shouted again, toning down the act to simmer.

"Lucy? Oh, we were at art school together." Another little smile. "Ages ago."

Always useful to know the name of the person whose party you've crashed.

"Those were the days," I replied, nodding wisely. "Still doing the art?"

"I wish. Theatre Admin. Small Scale Touring."

I had no idea what that was. "Paul," I said. As good a name as any for tonight. I reached out a hand.

"Jules." He shook mine weakly.

"Jules! In you get, mate." A space had miraculously opened and I pushed Jules towards it, squeezing in next to him.

"Hey pal, four Sambucas." I flashed the young barman my hard man stare and he scuttled off to get the bottle. Strictly speaking, Jules had been in front of me, but no one lives forever. Jules was still faffing about waving his £20 note towards no one in particular. The barman lined up the four glasses and sloppily filled them to the brim. Thrusting a tenner his way, I turned to Jules and pushed a shot into his non-twenty hand.

"Here's to small scale tearing!" I shouted, and downed my shot. Jules hesitated for a moment, then followed suit, only managing half. We'd be mates for a while now and if there was a bit of house party action later he'd come in handy. Picking up the last two shots, I nodded a closure at my new best friend and charted a course back to the target. There she was, talking to the dull looking woman in the baggy brown jumper. I can spot an outraged feminist type a mile off, so this would strictly be a quick flyby.

Coming up behind Ms. Blondie in stealth mode, I bent my index finger and ran the knuckle down her back from neck to bum. She turned, startled, and there was the open mouth again, the one I liked. I handed her the shot.

"Into the unknown!" I shouted over Duran Duran. I guessed these arty types would like something like that. Better than "down the hatch." We clinked and shot up together. Another good sign. I took her empty glass, fixed her the look, and turned back to the bar, just catching an unhappy glance from Brown Baggy. No matter. I'd ignore her now for a while and let the juices fester and boil.

I spent the next couple of tracks dancing moodily with myself in small "into the music" movements. Spying the birthday girl, now looking very unsteady and alone, I swung by the bar again for more magic shots. Looked like the barman was starting to wind down, not that he'd been a coiled spring in the first place. It was nearly midnight and I could see the party was beginning to die of natural causes. Keeping half an eye on my Blondie, who was still talking to Brown Baggy – fuck knows how they could speak over one of the less decent Madness songs at full volume – I made my move with the birthday girl, essential if I was going to get a piece of any house party action. I looked at her properly for the first time. She'd been on the cakes for a few years but had a huge chest and a little lopsided grin, which could be a symptom of dropsie or just a cute feature. I had my shots at the ready.

"Cheers to Birthday Lucy!" I yelled, holding out a glass.

She looked at me all befuddled but managed to grasp the drink with pudgy little fingers that ended in bite short red nails. I had a fleeting mental image of those tubby red digits closing around my cock and then decided it was never going to happen. Man has to draw the line somewhere.

"Cheers!" shouted Lucy and chugged it in one. I gave her a little smile and chugged mine too, but before I could swallow, she'd grabbed me by my love handles and pulled me close. A little Sambuca spurted from my mouth on impact and landed on her fringe, but she was too far gone to notice. A second later, she began pulling me around the room to *Monster Mash*, one of the least danceable tracks on the planet. I was cushioned from serious harm by the two airbags Lucy had deployed, but all the same it was getting outrageous. As we rotated, I caught glimpses of my Blondie and Brown Baggy laughing. I pushed down a wave of irritation as our helicoptering threatened to last to the end of Madness's greatest hits.

At long last birthday girl pulled away.

"That was nice," she bellowed. "Are you coming back to the house?"

Every experience has a silver lining in my book and here it was.

"Wild horses couldn't keep me away."

With that she did her lopsided grin and dragged me over to Blondie and friend.

"Get yer coats girls, I've pulled!" screamed Lucy, collapsing into giggles. I couldn't read the expression on Blondie's face but Brown Baggy looked distinctly sniffy.

Before any stilted conversations could begin, the house lights in the room went up and the music faded to mute.

"Noooo!" shrieked birthday girl dramatically. "It can't be midnight already!" Still holding me tight she swung us around and faced the now dreary looking room.

"Last one back to mine doesn't get any cider!" she yelled in a parade ground voice to the dozen or so remaining revellers. A less party looking bunch was hard to imagine. As well as Birthday girl, Blondie, Jules and Brown Baggy, there was a lanky white guy with specs already pulling on a cycling helmet, a pudgy Indian looking bloke with a T-shirt reading "Mine's a Ruddles", a severe girl with sensible shoes who already looked like a retired headmistress and a few others too unmentionable to mention. If I'd been called to pull together a last minute team for *University Challenge*, I'd have been well happy, but for a wild house party, it didn't look too promising. Then I looked at Blondie again and my cock gave a little twitch, just to remind me of my original plan.

Five minutes later, I found myself squeezed into the back seat of an aged Fiat Panda with birthday girl on one side and Brown Baggy on the other, driving at 19mph in top gear with Headmistress at the controls. There was a large transit van about nipples length from our bumper with lights on full beam right behind us, but no one apart from yours truly seemed to notice.

"You should report him to Trading Standards if his crisps are out of date," muttered Brown Baggy bitterly, maintaining a conversation between her and Birthday Girl that should have been drowned at birth.

"Crisps…" replied Birthday Girl groggily. She twisted her bulk even closer towards me, enclosing my elbow in soft flesh. "Have you ever dated a crisp, Paul?"

"No, but I've kissed some hula hoops," was the best I could come up with under the circumstances. But booze does strange things to people's sense of humour and she was suddenly laughing hysterically, giving my arm a vibrator like workout.

A loud blast and the transit van made its move, the driver leaving us with the image of his middle finger obscured by smoky exhaust.

"Macho idiot!" muttered Headmistress as our party carriage veered left into a side street and parked badly outside a tatty row of terraced houses where Mr Ruddles and Bike Helmet were standing awkwardly in each other's company. "Cider time," giggled Birthday Girl as she oozed out of the car and fumbled for house keys.

"Have you got any milk for tea, Lucy?" asked Bike Helmet.

"No way, Brian – Cider House rules!" She seemed mysteriously pleased with that and winked at me but Brian rolled his eyes. I was starting to warm to Lucy but this could get awkward. My mission, and I'd chosen to accept it, was Blondie.

We spilled into a gloomy hallway and then a bright living room. The two sofas looked inviting but I knew that once I sat down, chances were that Mr Ruddles or Headmistress would beeline next to me and start digging. Instead, I perched lightly on the sofa arm so I could access all areas. The room filled up, but Blondie was nowhere in sight. Before I could send out a search party, Lucy appeared with a bunch of posh French cider bottles between her tubby little fingers and passed them around.

"Cheers everyone – here's to 1972!" she yelled. She made to glug but suddenly realised the caps were still on. Huge giggles ensued and she bent double with a sort of drunken hysteria, releasing a mini fart as birthday gasses made their escape. This led Lucy to yet more merriment. I realised no one else was anywhere near as pissed as she was. They were all sitting around like twats with sealed bottles in their hands.

I opened mine with my teeth, a naff old party trick that was literally the only thing I'd learnt in the army. But it seemed to impress the assembled throng.

"Do me, do me!" squealed Lucy. I did her and then I did the others. There was a smattering of applause. It didn't compare to headlining at the O2, but it put me on a roll.

When I got to Headmistress, she looked less than certain but I grabbed her bottle anyway. Biting down for my final act, a sharp pain filled my mouth as a molar filed a complaint. Fuck! I winced, trying hard to ignore the agony as bits of filling went for a swim.

"Oh gosh, are you alright?" said Headmistress. I thought she was going to call matron.

"Yeah yeah, no problem." I needed to get out of there and re-group. Never look wounded. Also, where was Blondie? A quick spit and then some search and rescue was in order. I'd dicked about long enough with party games.

As I pushed past Lucy, she put her arm out to stop me.

"Where you going, honey?"

"I'm going out – and I may be some time." That old Captain Oates line always goes down well with the posh crowd, but quick as a flash, Lucy was there.

"Are you saying my house is cold?"

I was lost for words for just a second too long. Before I could come up with a Polar reply, she blew me a cider rich kiss, fluttered her eyes and turned back to talk to Mr Ruddles. I couldn't help a smile, but come on mate, action! As I got into the hallway, I could see that the front door was wide open. Not the best plan for this part of town, but maybe they were waiting for some more librarians or archeologists or whoever the fuck to pitch up. Before I could even think about closing it, I heard a thump, a tinkle of glass and a human moan coming from the kitchen. My brain began to make connections about my missing Blondie.

Pushing open the kitchen door, I was greeted by the nightmare vision of Bike Helmet's pale buttocks attending to the urgent affairs of whatever mystery lay between the spread legs of Blondie, who was perched precariously on the dirty kitchen work surface. I took in the broken glass on the floor and then up to see Blondie's open mouth uttering small animal sounds that I had hoped would be mine alone to decipher. Losses to be cut, I turned to go, but Blondie's sex closed eyes suddenly sprung open and fixed me with a stare that nailed my feet to the floor. Then her mouth broke into a grin, a giggle, a hysterical laugh, pushing Bike Helmet out of his cycle path. He twisted around to face me, an outraged expression beginning to form on his face. I'm normally pretty cool in these situations, but the fact that he was still wearing both helmet and gloves freaked me out. I reversed quickly out of the room. Time to leave.

As I passed the living room, I heard Lucy's voice shouting, then a male voice saying, 'Fuck off bitch.' It didn't sound like either a librarian or an archaeologist but it wasn't any business of mine who she'd invited. When I got to the front door, I stopped. I'm not a total cunt, although there's a long list of people who might disagree. Something was clearly wrong, judging by all the extra shouting.

Taking a deep breath and puffing myself up, I pushed open the living room door. It seemed the party had three new guests and it was clear they hadn't received embossed invitations. Lucy was facing off with a young white guy who was at the higher end of the macho scale judging by his bad tattoos. Next to him was a larger and older black geezer, chewing gum and sporting a thousand yard stare. And comfy on the sofa was a huge fat kid of about nineteen, who'd grabbed a bowl of crisps and was stuffing his face in a way you don't at your grandma's. Poor Jules was almost out of sight under the fat kid's shoulder.

My entrance seemed to freeze the action. My ex always used to say I could suck the air out of a room, and for once this was a plus.

"All right lads," I said in my deepest most casual voice.

"Paul, they're stealing our drinks and they won't go," said Lucy forcefully, but I could hear the fear under her words. And it was true – both Tattoo man and Thousand Yard had cardboard packs of posh cider in their hands. The room was silent for a moment, apart from the manic crisp crunching coming from the sofa.

I knew I'd have to front this somehow. I scoured the room for allies. Jules was trapped in fat, Mr Ruddles was shaking quietly to himself, Headmistress was looking at her feet. I couldn't rely on Bike Helmet and Blondie to ride up and save the day. Only Brown Baggy and Lucy looked like they had any fight in them, but we weren't talking SAS.

"Tell you what lads, you take a couple of bottles each on us and be on your way," I said with a small smile, but with what I hoped was just a hint of menace.

"Tell you what, Pauuuul, why don't you go fuck yourself," replied Tattoo man, not unreasonably, before moving so close into my personal space I could identify the gaps in his daily brushing routine.

My UN peacekeeping tactics exhausted, I brought my knee up hard into his groin and as he folded, I pushed him towards Thousand Yard. The collision sent both of them spiralling into the sofa and onto Fat Boy and Jules. I knew from my less than distinguished bar fighting career that I had to take the upper hand quick, otherwise I was fucked.

"Hit him with your bottle!" I yelled at Brown Baggy, and to my amazement she complied, bashing the rising Thousand Yard right on the head as he rose to take his revenge. He sat down again, stunned. This was the dangerous one I realised. Grabbing him, I pulled him to his feet, twisted his arm round his back and pushed him out the living room, clipping him on the frame as I went. Rushing him down the hallway, I propelled him through the still open front door. He careered into the wing mirror of the Fiat Panda and sat down heavily on the pavement. Running back into the house, I slammed the front door behind me. One down, two to go. Keeping up the energy – I knew it wouldn't last much longer - I pushed my way back into the living room, grabbed an empty cider bottle and smashed it on the cast iron woodburner. Just in time, as Tattoo man was about to punch Brown Baggy and Fat Boy was now on his feet, looking like the before in an extreme weight watchers ad, minus the smile.

"Out out out!" I yelled, pushing the broken bottle towards the two men who now resembled more Laurel and Hardy than two South London hard nuts.

"Lucy, call Leroy and the boys and tell 'em to get the fuck over here," I shouted, and like a good actor, she started to fumble for her phone. Teamwork!

I waved the bottle menacingly and the lads started to see sense. Little did they know there was no way I was going to cut them. I really couldn't do any more time.

"Take it easy man," muttered Tattoo as I herded them towards the front door. Fat Boy looked dazed, his mouth still open and partially full of crisp goo. As they spilled out into the street, I could see no sign of Thousand Yard. That could read both ways. Just then Lucy came to the front door waving her phone.

"They're on their way," she shouted. Good girl. Could have used her in Kosovo. The bars that is.

I pushed Lucy back inside and slammed the front door. Then I heard the kitchen door creak open. I held my breath. I wasn't sure I had any go left in me. But it was Bike Helmet and Blondie.

"Thought we heard some shouting," said Bike Helmet. "Everything OK?"

"Yeah," both Lucy and I said at exactly the same time. She caught my eye and started to giggle again, and this time I joined in. It was a nice giggle but if we kept it up it could get out of hand.

"Well, Jocelyn and I have to shoot," said Bike Helmet. "She's got an Ofsted next week, so, you know."

After another pointless pleasantry or two they headed for the front door. I opened it for them and peeked out, but the coast was clear. As they squeezed past Jocelyn gave me a little peck on the cheek and a half smile but I was too wired to respond. Besides, at that moment, the rest of the party poopers appeared. Headmistress was going to drive everyone home. After some mutterings about how we really should call the Police they too trouped out.

Then Brown Baggy appeared in the hallway with a poker in her hand.

"They might be back Lucy, so I'm not going to leave you," she said.

"Three of us, three of them then," said Lucy. I liked their style.

Later, with Brown Baggy sleeping in one of the bedrooms, Lucy and I fucked on the sofa. It was surprisingly good. "In the morning, you really must tell me who the hell you are," whispered Lucy before we dozed off. I worried about that for a moment, then decided I'd cross that bridge when the time came. I always did. I snuggled closer and drifted off to sleep thinking about fighting, crisps and pudgy little fingers with bite red nails.

Afterword

Thank you for reading our stories. If you've loved them - or if you've loathed them - please post a review on Amazon.